Target Shy & Sexy
L. J. Martin

The Repairman Series No. 5
Target Shy & Sexy
L. J. Martin

WOLFPACK
PUBLISHING
— EST 2013 —

Print Edition
Copyright 2015 L. J. Martin

Wolfpack Publishing
6032 Wheat Penny Avenue
Las Vegas, NV 89122

ISBN 978-1-62918-307-7

Prologue

No one could have been more surprised, after returning from a very tough job in Montana which ended in a week's fly fishing with my buddy—which wasn't so tough—to find a call waiting from a former employer.

Tammy Houston, rapidly becoming a very famous, very successful, country and western singer.

The hell of it is, the last time I did a gig for Tammy she fired me and it cost me fourteen grand to pay for the medical bills of a couple of young eco-terrorists who tried to defend a smartass kid who threw paint on what the destructive little bitch thought was a fur coat. One lousy broken arm, only a slightly broken jaw, and the assholes deserved it. So I was out lots of dough and a month doing community service in a Seattle soup kitchen.

I'd snatched the wrist of the hippy girl who'd just thrown paint on Tammy's fur coat. The hell of it was the coat was faux fur and not that expensive. That didn't keep me from turning the young lady—if you can call a rude young hippie girl a lady—over my knee, right outside the Gaucho restaurant on 2nd Street in downtown Seattle, and tanning her butt until she bawled like a baby.

Of course I spent the night in the hoosegow…not for the spanking, but for breaking the jaw of one long-hair and the arm of another who decided to come to the property-destroying hippie girl's rescue. I take umbrage when someone is stupid enough to pull a two-inch blade penknife on me and broke that one's arm to cure him of said stupidity, and the jaw of the other as he called me a son of a bitch and a cocksucker and tried to kick me in the gonads. "Son of a bitch" I don't mind so much as I'm sure he was not really casting dispersions on my mom. My nads? Now that's another matter altogether. And a cocksucker? Now I take real umbrage at that. It was clearly a case of self-defense, however Judge Polkinghorn, who I'd like to poke in the eye, didn't agree.

It doesn't pay to beat up on rich-kid-liberals in Seattle, particularly when one's daddy is on the city council.

No good deed goes unpunished.

I also paid a five thousand dollar fine and did four weeks community service in a Seattle soup kitchen serving goulash to guys who drove up in BMW's. Truthfully not all of them drove up in anything, as many actually needed a hot meal. Having never begged, I'm not positive, but suspect it's much easier to work for a living. All that said, I know some guys who came back from Iraq, as I did, who were too screwed up to hold a job. I gave the vets an extra portion.

I even made a few new friends while on the job, including a priest, Father Sean O'Donnel, who runs the joint. I traded some carpentry work—hanging doors—for a basement room while I paid my penance. I could have afforded a nearby hotel room, but one adds to life's experiences as one can…and I did.

As it turned out the judge did me a favor with the community service as I recognized a guy for whom I was dishing up some slop; a guy who'd skipped a hundred grand bail in Las Vegas. Carrying a bail enforcement badge—thirty five bucks will get you one—I called the bondsman, got a contract, put the guy face down on the sidewalk after his next bummed bowl of soup and collected a twenty grand recovery fee for hauling him into the same lockup I'd recently left.

God works in mysterious ways.

Tammy still owes me for that week's work. I was not holding my breath waiting to collect, however it seems I'm now in demand. And she's a little more interested in my specialties, as someone knocked a great big chunk out of her fireplace in the multi-million dollar condo she now occupies. Cops said a 50 cal mag did the dirty deed from a thousand yards away.

The long-hairs' medical bills cost me fourteen thousand, so, after my three grand premium to a local bondsman, the fine, a few expenses, and the medical bills, I came out about three grand in the hole.

Living in the basement of a homeless shelter was not such a bad gig, as my primary residence, my second home, and my third and fourth are ministorage rooms…or at least had been until I invested in a 250 Ford truck and a camper. I also own a van, which is a necessity for the occasional bail enforcement—bounty hunting—I do. One occasionally needs tie downs and room to hook up a perp or two.

Of course I have an iPhone, and a half dozen throw away phones, so I really didn't need to drop by my buddy Pax Weatherwax's office. But he does have the best coffee in town, and the price is right.

Pax owns an Internet Service Provider company with offices in six cities, and keeps me out of trouble and loaded with information on clients and bad guys. Information that is probably just short of what the NSA could procure. He's really, really, really good at what he does.

And he's also my best friend, as we rambled through Desert Storm together, kept each other alive, and would have thrown ourselves on a grenade to save the other, if need be. As it is, he has one leg an inch and a half shorter than the other thanks to dragging me out of a street singing with AK47 rounds and taking one through the thigh.

He still is the best man with a .308 I know—Marine sniper trained—and damn good with any other weapon. I don't want him after me, short leg or no.

I take the stairs up the back way to his two-car garage sized office, his back looking at the Vegas strip a few blocks distant, and catch him with his nose in some software manual.

"Hey!" I shout, and he jumps a foot.

"You son of a bitch," he stammers.

"Watch your mouth, fat boy," I say with a laugh.

"Fuck you. I can take you in anything but a foot race."

"I need to use a phone and want to put my butt in an easy chair to do so."

"Good, I'm busy here."

So I plop down in a far corner, grab the phone, and dial the area code 310 number Tammy left.

"Miss Houston's residence," the male voice answers.

"Funny, that's who I called." I'm feeling a little sassy as she's had to phone me, and I know it grates at her.

"May I say who's calling?"

"Mr. Michael Reardon, you may say."

"Is she expecting you?" he asks, his voice slightly more gruff.

"She might be expecting twins for all I know. I'm returning her call."

"You're a little flippant." His voice is even more gruff.

"You've got one minute to get her on the phone, or I'm hanging up. One more time, Sherlock, I'm returning her call."

"Right, hold on." I know he's put a hand over the receiver, but can hear him nonetheless. "Some smartass says he's returning your call. Michael Reardon."

It's far less than five seconds when she picks up the phone, and she's slightly out of breath like she's run to grab it.

"Hi, Mike."

"Hi, Miss Houston," I say, slightly tongue in cheek.

"You know it's Tammy to you."

"Okay, Tammy. So long as I'm not working for you, it's Tammy. What's up?"

"I need your help."

I have to chuckle a little. "As I recall, you don't like my help."

"That was when I was young and naive. I've learned some things."

"Two years ago you were naive and now you're mature?"

"I've learned a lot."

"Okay," I sigh. "What do you need?"

"Protection. I'll explain it when you get here."

"Hell, there are a thousand guys out there—"

"I want you."

"You owe me for a week's work. You dropped me in the grease and cost me twenty grand."

"So, I was paying you five grand a week and cost you twenty grand, so a twenty-five thousand retainer will get you back to work."

"Hardly. That's what you owe me. I now get ten grand a week for my services and require a two week retainer."

"Ten grand…who do you think you are? Merle Haggard?"

"Nope, I've never done time in the big house."

She's quiet for a moment, then, "So, twenty thousand will get you here?"

"Plus the twenty-five grand you owe me."

"You drive a tough bargain."

"And I'm very tough on people who mean to do my clients harm. And if Forbes knows, you're knocking down five mil a month and that alone will attract some scumbags."

"Yeah, but I have a lot of expenses." She's silent for a moment. "Will you be at this number? I've got it on my phone here."

"I'll be here until I take a buddy to supper. Maybe an hour or so."

"I'll call you back."

"Whatever," I say. I saw that in some hot shot young Hollywood movie, so I guess it's the thing to say to twenty-five-year-olds, almost twenty years my junior.

"I'll call. I've got to clear it with Emory."

"Whatever....or maybe I should say, whomever." There, I've said it twice. Am I hip, or what?

So I hang up. It's good to have money in the bank and be independent.

She calls back in fifteen minutes, with an affirmative.

Chapter One

I'd returned Tammy's call on a Friday and she asked me to be front and center at her condo in Beverly Hills at 9:00 AM on Monday morning to meet with her manager, Emory, and get up to speed on the job. He was to have a check for me in the amount of forty-five grand, the twenty-five she'd cost me and the twenty grand retainer.

Not as bad as Sunday night, still even Monday morning is a terrible time to drive from Vegas to L.A., as you're taking your life in your hands with the last of the weekend traffic. Those folks may have knocked down the free booze at the tables right up until they climbed in their SUVs and headed for the City of the Angels. So I climb in my classic red and white Vette at three AM. The drunks are still on the highway, but fewer of them and you have a little room to duck and dodge. As I'm not applying for a job at IBM I wear a soft brown pullover, black Wranglers, and black Reeboks. When Tammy was young, two years ago, she required her security to be in coat and tie. So we looked like security—ties, ear buds, and serious demeanors. Easy to spot from a hundred yards. I hope she's outgrown that affectation.

The condo is in a high rise—at least twenty stories—on Wilshire actually in Westwood. I guess Tammy thinks Beverly Hills sounds more prestigious as she said the latter, and, after all, it's only a stone's throw. I guess the condo building at twenty stories, as Tammy's address is No. 2001. With, of course, a three-hundred-pound guard—with simian brows and a low growl to match—at the entrance to the parking garage. He informs me that he does not have me on the visitor list, so "...please back it up and let me see your tail as you disappear." He's a real card for a knuckle dragger. I find a parking place on the street three blocks away, and call the number Tammy left for me earlier.

No answer.

I'm not anal about much, but being on time...in fact doing what I say I'm going to do...is on top the list.

The entry to the building is lined with video cameras, and like the garage there's an attendant, a doorman behind a counter in the foyer. He's a little classier than the parking lot gorilla, with a pinned collar and perfect crease in the tie. The foyer is marble—floor and walls—and the ceiling is brass with tiny inset LED lighting. There's a ten by ten foot brass relief of a number of old stars—Bing Crosby, Elvis, Sinatra, Al Jolson, and others—on one wall and a smaller one on the face of the counter, the counter itself is brass. There's one bench, uncomfortable cold marble, for those asked to wait.

I'm not surprised to find the large glass entry door locked and a video camera and press-to-talk box on the wall nearby. When I try the door the well-dressed guard points at the brass box so I comply.

"Here to see Tammy Houston's people, have an appointment. I'm Mike Reardon."

Without looking at a calendar, he replies. "I have you on the calendar." And buzzes me in.

As I head for the elevator, he adds. "I don't think there's anyone up there. You a cop?"

Where'd he get that? I glance down at the way I'm dressed, brown shirt and all, and say with all seriousness, "Undercover with UPS."

He nods. I guess there's no IQ test for even well-dressed doormen.

It's a fast elevator to the penthouse floor, where I observe as I step out, there are only two penthouse apartments. Tammy's wasting no time blowing her five mil a month. I guess she's never studied the phrase "fame is fleeting."

Maybe already flown.

But I'm stopped short. The door with 2001 in brass letters has yellow crime tape crisscrossed across the opening.

Neither the parking garage attendant nor the doorman mentioned the fact the place was sealed up…but that explains the doorman asking if I was a cop.

Nonetheless, I ring the bell and can hear the notes to Tammy's first big hit, Houston Hottie in lieu of the standard two tone.

No one answers. Which does not surprise me as cops don't normally seal someone inside a crime scene.

Not to be easily dissuaded I return to the brass-accented foyer and as I leave wave my phone at the guard. "I'm ten minutes early. The detective said he'd be a little late. I'll be right back."

My well-worn lock pick set and rubber gloves are in the Vette. These days fingerprints are less important as there are probably a half dozen video cameras trained on me between my parking spot and the building, and some real good close-ups taken from front door and foyer cameras, and as I felt no need I've not employed any facial disguise. Still, I don't want the absolute proof of prints left at the scene.

No, I don't think my check will be waiting on a kitchen counter, but I do want to see what the hell's up. This time the door guard buzzes me in as I top the entry stairs.

I'm operating on the premise that the "do not enter" on the crime scene tape is advice, not an order. And, after all, I've been invited by the owner occupant.

It takes me all of thirty seconds to pop the entry lock, and another full minute on the dead bolt. It takes longer to work my way through the crisscross crime scene tape without ripping it off the jamb.

The condo is at least six thousand square feet with living room, kitchen, expansive dining room, powder room, two guest rooms with baths, and a patio larger than the average city apartment on the entry floor and a winding stairway to a second floor. I do find the chunk out of the fireplace, which was the reason I was called in the first instance. If it came through the sliding glass door leading out to the patio, it's been repaired. After seeing nothing else out of order on that floor, I ascend the stairway to an interior balcony with four doors, one of which is a double door and I presume the master.

And I'm right as I enter to see a bed about the size of a soccer field.

Opposite the headboard is a floor-to-ceiling window wall, and I quickly spot the reason for the crime scene tape.

The bad news: a perfect bullet hole, head high in the glass, with cracks spider-webbing out at least a foot all around. Someone was serious, as it again appears to be a fifty caliber.

Am I too late to protect Miss Houston? I have to consciously relax my jaw as my teeth are beginning to ache. No matter how young and ignorant Tammy had been during our first mutual experience, I liked her and would hate to think of her shot by some Neanderthal stalker…or anyone else for that matter.

The good news: no bloodstains anywhere in the bedroom.

The ceiling is at least ten feet high, and the first thing I look for is a bullet hole in the opposite wall, and it's not hard to locate as it's near the ceiling next to the bed, with an orange felt-tip pen circle around where a bullet's been dug out of the wall by some CSI dude.

So the shot came at an upward angle, as is not surprising firing at a twenty story condo. Even though there are a half-dozen other buildings within a half mile of the condo, it's fairly simple to determine the likelihood of where the shot came from and I note the location of a twelve to fifteen story building a few hundred yards to the west, also fronting on Wilshire Boulevard. Its rooftop is a couple of stories lower than Tammy's building, thus the up angle.

There's no question in my mind that LAPD or whoever is the "power that be" in Westwood has worked the building from which the shot obviously came, so I don't bother creeping that location.

It's more important to discover what happened to Tammy.

And to have breakfast. I contemplate better over a plate of flapjacks.

Every once in a while I splurge with calories, and I know a spot close by. Mon Amour Café is only a couple of blocks and has crepes that will break even an old country boy who loves flapjacks into a cold sweat. I grab an L.A. Times on the way in and am only two bites into their "original crepe" that comes with bananas and strawberries, slathered with whipped cream, when I find an article in the local section. "Country Star Houston Flees Attempted Murder." The article goes on to say after a gunshot was fired into her condo, she disappeared into the night with her entourage. The cops have no clue who tried to drop our diva.

After dusting off the original for breakfast and a chocolate one for dessert, I am ready to get to work. Don't go to this joint for service, only if you love crepes and can stand creeps.

Once settled back in my Vette, I call my buddy Pax in Vegas.

"Hey, I need a little keyboard magic."

"Make it quick, I'm busy."

"Do I need to find a new best friend?"

"Fuck you, Farley. Ask."

"Somebody tried to dust my new client before she becomes my new client. See what you can find out about what happened and to where she might have flown. She's hiding out and not answering the number I have. You might try her manager for a phone number, some guy named Emory something."

"I'll put Sol on it. He can be your next best friend."

"Good, he's better than you anyway."

"Sit on it, Sunshine, where the sun don't shine."

"I'll stand by."

I read the rest of my paper, and it's a good thing I read fast as my phone buzzes and it's Sol, who's one of those twenty-five-year-old computer genius types who's worked for Pax since he was a teenager.

"She has a place in Malibu." He gives me an address near Point Dume State Park. "The land line there is unlisted but it's 555-6720."

"Also 310, right."

"Right. And her manager, Emory Coogan, is 805-555-3433."

"I owe you a tall cold one."

"How about a five-foot-two blonde one."

"Drinks I can do, Sol. You got to take care of your own love life."

"But you're so much better at it."

"You're in Vegas, my man. A blonde on every street corner."

"Yeah, but I don't pay for it."

"Thanks for the help."

"De nada."

So I dial the Malibu land line. No answer, get a machine, and leave a message. So I dial Coogan and likewise get a recording and leave a message.

I can be there in thirty minutes, traffic allowing, so head out. It's a great drive and a great day, so I put the top down on the Vette and enjoy it.

Nothing like a drive up the California coast on a beautiful day with an ocean breeze and California King Gulls circling overhead. And the plethora of young starlets, or starlet wannabes cruising by.

And I'm happy, until I work my way through the maze of roads at Dume Point and arrive at Tammy's ocean front address…and there's yellow crime scene tape strung all over the driveway.

A half-dozen L.A. County sheriff cars.

An ambulance.

What the hell?

Target Shy & Sexy

Chapter Two

I duck under the crime scene tape and am immediately confronted by a deputy. I flash my bail enforcement officer's badge at him and being a young guy new to the job he doesn't take a hard look and waves me on by. It's sometimes a wonder what thirty-five bucks for a chunk of brass can do for you.

A gurney is loaded with a very big, blond Nordic type, who is being hoisted by a couple of EMT's who look about to bust a gut trying to get it up so it can be rolled into the back of the bus. So I pause long enough to get a good look at the passenger and help them.

While I'm doing so, a plainclothes guy walks over.

"Who are you?" he asks.

As soon as we get the gurney up, I nod and extend my hand. "Mike Reardon. I'm security for Miss Houston. What's happened here?"

The guy does accept the handshake. Then asks in a cold tone. "You got some I.D.?"

As I'm showing the pudgy rumpled cop—jelly stains on his yellow power tie—my badge wallet which also contains my legitimate Nevada driver's license, another guy of equal weight to the two-hundred-sixty-pound guy on the gurney walks over. He's no Nordic type, more swarthy Italian.

"This guy is not Tammy's security," he snaps, with a bit of a Southern drawl, and the plainclothes cop places a hand on the semi-auto clipped to his belt.

"Miss Houston hired me over the phone," I say.

"You're Mike Reardon?" the swarthy dude asks, and the cop relaxes a little.

"I am."

"You're not needed any longer." He's smiling with only one side of his mouth, more a smirk than a smile.

"And you are?"

"I'm Emory Coogan, Tammy's manager." Not Italian, black Irish, I conclude.

"So, where's Miss Houston?"

The cop steps closer. "She's been abducted, forty five minutes ago. We've got an APB out."

"So," Coogan repeats, "you're not needed. Sorry you made the trip." He says it, but doesn't mean it. Then he turns back to the plainclothes guy. "Detective, can you show Reardon off the property."

The cop gives Coogan a look that says I ain't your butler, and doesn't move.

"Hold on, hotshot," I say to Coogan, feeling the heat creep up my neck. "Miss Houston and I go way back—"

"Yeah," he says with a slight guffaw, "she fired your ass a couple of years ago, right before she hired Butch."

"And she hired me back a couple of days ago."

"She has a contract waiting for you inside, and a check, but you're not getting it now. I'm in charge of Tammy's affairs, so beat a trail back to Vegas."

I bite my lip, wishing I could bust his. But rather merely nod and turn to the detective. "I didn't get your name?"

"I didn't offer it, but it's Adamson, Detective Howard Adamson."

"Thanks. And who's the boy in the bus?"

"That's Horrigan. Butch Horrigan. He got blindsided and stun-gunned and hit his head on the way down. He's going in for observation."

"How's he play into this?"

"You should know if Miss Houston hired you. He's the head of security for her."

I nod, and give Coogan a disgusted look, and start for the crime scene tape, and can't help a little sarcasm. "I guess he doesn't give good head. I can show myself out."

"Humph," is all I get from Coogan, but Adamson calls after me.

"Hey," he steps over and hands me a card. "Call me this afternoon."

"Will do."

"Yeah," Coogan says, "call him from Vegas."

I have the urge to give swarthy Coogan the middle finger, maybe extended but more likely stuck in his eye...but neither is considered professional.

As I head for the crime scene tape and my Vette beyond, I hear footsteps behind and a ladylike voice calls out, "Mike Reardon."

I turn, and see it's a tall brunette, lithe but bulges in all the right places, with laser-blue eyes that would melt metal. She's about Tammy's age. "Yes, ma'am."

"He's leaving," Coogan's voice is raised from fifty feet away.

"I'll only be a moment," the brunette says, over her shoulder, then turns back to me and extends a well-manicured and polished hand. "I'm Tyler...Tyler Thompson. I handle Tammy's bookings and travel, and we're good friends. She told me lots about you."

Tyler slips me a card as she speaks and I stuff it in a back pocket of the Wranglers as Coogan is heading this way, imitating a freight train.

"He's leaving," he snaps, and with a little too rough a hand drags Tyler Thomson back a couple of steps. Coogan keeps moving as if he's expecting me to give ground, but instead I step into him and give him a sound chest bump as if someone on our team just made a touchdown.

"Oof," he manages, and before he can get anything else out, I give him a stiff one-finger poke in the plexus and he "oofs" again, and back steps, a little wide eyed. I think he's going to swing and am hoping he does, but he reconsiders as he's still trying to catch his breath from the finger jab.

So with a voice low and serious, I say, "You know something, Coogan, had that lady not acted like she was used to you jerking her around, I'd be standing over you with one foot on your chest and you swallowing teeth and blood. I'm not much for some asshole pushing women around. And I'm tempted to drop you nonetheless."

"Who the fuck do you think you are? Get the hell off this property," he stammers.

I turn to Tyler. "You okay, Miss Thompson?"

"I'm fine, thank you." She says, then, unseen by Coogan, gives me the telephone receiver signal with thumb and little finger extended from mouth to ear, and mouths, "Call me."

I nod. And move toward the tape, then stop as I duck under and look back at Coogan, who's standing with his arms thrown back as if he's about to charge across the twenty-five feet separating us.

So I invite him. "Sure you don't need some help, fat man?"

"Not from you, dipshit. Beat a trail back to Vegas."

So I do. No check here. I'm all the way down to Sunset and thinking of stopping and messing around town until I can go to Dan Tana's for some great Italian before heading back to Vegas, before my adrenaline wears off.

Then it begins to creep into my pea brain that Tammy hired me so only Tammy can fire me. And what kind of guy am I who ignores a woman so obviously in peril, if still alive? I presume this is a kidnapping for ransom, so she's a damsel needing rescue.

Money or no, check or no, I gotta turn around.

She wanted my help, and even though I gave her a bad time, she employed me with a verbal contract...and like I said before, I always do what I say I'm going to do.

And I said I'd take on the job of protecting Tammy Houston.

Target Shy & Sexy

Chapter Three

As I'm driving back I poke the voice activation on my hands free and call Pax.

Rosie, his receptionist and one of my favorite ladies, all two hundred pounds of her, answers with her normally cheerful voice. "Weatherwax Internet Services."

"How can you make even that sound so sexy?" I ask.

And she giggles, as I knew she would, then answers, "Hey, big boy, when are you bringing me some more of those wonderful chocolate truffles?"

"Sorry, I'm on the coast. Why are you answering the boss's cell phone?"

"He went to the gym and accidently left his cell on my desk."

"Old age is hell. Sol around?"

"He is, but you'd rather talk to me."

"No doubt, but there's a damsel in distress and I need him badly."

"Okay, you're no fun. Except for the damsel maybe."

"Work is hell, and one must sacrifice. Sol, please."

"Sol, the hack man," he answers as I normally address him.

"Hey, somebody snatched my almost client. The L.A. sheriff has an APB out on a van. Find out what you can, financial, etcetera, on all the players. Tammy Houston; Emory Coogan, her manager; Tyler Thompson, her travel and booking person, a lady person...and a lug named Butch Horrigan, supposedly her security."

"You got it. You want me to hack into L.A. County?"

"Not yet. Let's not risk it until it's imperative. I've got a contact there."

"Go get 'em, Mike."

As soon as he's off, I dial the number Tyler Thompson gave me. She answers.

"Tyler."

"Hi, kid. It's Mike Reardon."

"Oh...oh, hi Genny."

"Can't talk?"

"Not even a little."

"Where'd they take Horrigan?"

"Oh, yeah, we've had a hell of a day. Somebody kidnapped Tammy...but you've got to keep it quiet. And Butch was taken to U.C.L.A. med center with a busted head."

"Thanks, I'll call you later."

"Cool."

I hear a gruff voice in the background as she's hanging up. "Shut that up..."

So, I'm off to the university hospital in Westwood. Not too far from Dan Tana's in Beverly Hills, and some high class Italian.

Before I turn off onto the far west end of the infamous Sunset Boulevard, my phone vibrates and I see it's from Sol, and his first report on the folks inquired about. I pull into a small Brentwood strip center with a Starbucks, dig my laptop out and open the attachments. I go straight to the Butch Horrigan file. Born Benjamin Horrigan, first nickname Benny, took on Butch after serving a three-year term in Tehachapi State Prison for assault on a police officer. He served the full three as it appears there was no good behavior. In fact he was tried again for assault while in prison due to a prison riot, but was found innocent for lack of proof. Born in Fresno, California, he did three years at Fresno State, a college not a prison, and played tackle on a winning football team until he was thrown out of school for breaking some kid's arm and using a beer bottle on another at a fraternity party he'd crashed. He obviously thinks of himself a tough guy. Well, the tough guy wasn't as tough as the mace and whoever hauled off his client.

It's not a very interesting story, maybe it'll be more interesting from the horse's mouth.

I park in a multi-story parking garage near the hospital and go to the desk to discover he's still in the emergency room...typical of today's hospitals. There are probably forty illegal aliens in the queue in front of him. That, too, is typical of today's southwest U.S. hospitals. I have nothing against folks trying to better themselves; I just wish they wouldn't climb on the backs of those of us here legally just after swimming the Rio Grande or jumping the very porous fence. And that wish includes stopping them from voting illegally for those who'll continue to buy their votes with giveaways.

The girl at the ER desk asks my interest in Mr. Horrigan, and I tell her I'm his half-brother, and as he's in a cubicle awaiting a doc I am pointed to number eight. At least he got as far as a bed. I'm no stranger to hospitals, have had more than my share of wounds; but I never get used to the Lysol or bleach smell, the groans and moans, and the painted directional stripes on the floor...knowing one—probably the black one—leads to the morgue.

I hate the places.

I push my way through the curtains and see our boy flat on his back, and his stomach stands as high or maybe a little higher than his chest...this boy is no five percent body fat as a good scrapper might be. More than likely he's good at cleaning up the scraps from the table.

His eyes are closed, but snap open when I address him.

"How you doin' Benny boy?"

He begins to raise his head, but then collapses back to his pillow. "Who the hell is that, calling me Benny?"

"You haven't been Benny since Tehachapi, or when?"

This time he manages to hold his head up and focus on me. "Who the hell are you? You a cop?"

"Nope. I'm the bodyguard Tammy should have had."

"Fuck you, they maced me."

"When you opened the door and stood there like a gob of suet. How about taking a peek through the peep hole first? It's hard to get mace to penetrate oak and glass."

"Fuck you, I'm her bodyguard."

"And you may be guarding a dead body by the time you get out of this meat processing plant."

He's silent for a moment, then speaks with his head down flat on the pillow, his eyes at the ceiling. "So, you're gonna look for her?"

"No, I'm gonna find her, alive I hope. Why'd they take her?"

"You gotta ask Coogan."

"I'm asking you."

"Coogan."

"You have any idea who they were?"

"Fuck no."

So I reach over and put the flat of my hand on the knot on the side of his head. "Do you suppose if I press hard on this lump I'll push the mush you call brains out of your nose?"

He grabs my wrist, but I pry his thumb away with my other hand, and not gently.

He winces. "I'm yelling for the doc."

"Too late by the time he gets here, not that he could do anything about it nonetheless. I guess he'll get here in time to clean up the mess. So, why'd they take Tammy?"

I reach again for the knot. "Oh, fuck, don't push."

"Why'd they take Tammy?"

"I'm gonna kick your ass when I get out of here...ooww. Fuck!"

"Why'd they take Tammy, tough guy?"

"They said they wanted their money. Now stop pushing."

"What money?"

"Fuck, I don't know. I don't owe them no money."

"And Tammy does?"

"Tammy don't handle the money...her money...Coogan does."

"So Coogan owes them?"

"Ask Coogan. Doc!" he yells.

"We'll talk again when you get out of here, if the docs don't kill you."

"Doc!" he yells, then, "nurse!"

I have to laugh. He sounds a little like a six year old yelling for his mama.

"See you around, killer," I say, as I exit, passing a nurse running his way.

As soon as I get back to the parking garage, I have to hack the flavor of beach and hospital out of my throat.

On my way back to the Vette, I dial Coogan and it goes to answering. So I again dial Tyler, and this time she sounds a little more relaxed.

"So, pretty lady, how about you and I getting together and talking?" I ask.

"Can't, I'm headed back to the apartment in Westwood."

"It's taped up."

"They said I could get back in this evening."

"How about some great Italian at Dan Tana's?"

"Oh, I love Dan Tana's. What time?"

"How about eight. I'll get us a reservation."

"Eight it is."

Chapter Four

She wanders in slowly, seductively, eyeing the room.

I'm in a booth in a far corner and jump up to meet her. The place is red leather and dark wood, quiet waiters who move like specters but are always close at hand and great food and drinks.

It all reminds me of film noir, Humphrey Bogart from the late thirties or forties. And she fits right in, even looks a little like Lauren Bacall. Basic black cocktail dress, nice black high-heels sans the platforms many girls wear—she's tall enough—with a small buckle on each crusted with faux diamonds, rhinestones I presume. Her legs are bare...Bacall would have worn nylons. The one-faux-diamond-rhinestone-thick belt she wears drapes on slim hips like an oversized tennis bracelet, but there's enough flare there to say she's lady shaped, and it's obvious she's braless and they stand up nicely without the shoulder-slings. A very, very nice package and the plethora of men in the place seem to agree as all eyes follow as she winds between tables to meet me halfway.

"You clean up nice," she offers, and I put a hand on the small of her back and escort her to our corner booth. She slips in and rather than take the side of the curved booth facing her, I slip in beside her.

"Thanks," I reply, "but I'm surprised I can answer and you look so good I'm tongue-tied."

She smiles, and with a sexy tone says, "Thanks," then laughs, "Don't say tongue unless you mean it," then adds as my mouth goes dry, "Cozy."

"You bet." I say, but I'm thinking about the tongue remark. Who wouldn't? But I add, "No telling how intimate the conversation might get so we don't want to be overheard."

She laughs. "You don't waste any time."

"It wasn't me made the tongue crack, to risk a pun."

"Like I said, you don't waste time."

"Dilly-dally has never been my strong suit."

"And I bet long-term relationships have never been your strong suit either."

I feign being hurt. "Wow, the lady judges me before we've had our first drink together."

"Speaking of drinks, what's that you're having?"

"Jack rocks, I usually have it neat but want my wits about me on a first date."

"Date? I thought this was business."

Now it's my turn to laugh. "Yeah, it would have been until you showed up in that luscious-fitting black piece. That doesn't say biz to me."

"Just so I know."

"Speaking of business, let's get a little biz out of the way."

"How about I get a Manhattan first."

The waiter is already on his way, so I put in her order, "Manhattan up, two cherries." Then I turn back to her. "So who do you think has run off with your boss?"

She's quiet for a second and I think she's going to break into tears. Then offers, "I have no idea. All celebs have stalkers but they usually operate alone. Three guys hit the front door and dragged her away from a poolside chaise lounge in a bikini."

"After they dropped the bodyguard."

"Yes."

"Where was Coogan?"

"In the John. He came out and seemed a little surprised to see Butch on the floor rolling around."

"Seemed?"

Again she's quiet for a moment. Then she sighs deeply before continuing. "He's been under a lot of pressure lately."

"Horrigan?"

"No, Emory."

"Why?"

"He doesn't talk much."

"I caught a little electricity between you two. You and he have a...a thing going?"

She's given to thinking before she speaks, and does again. She bats her dark lids at me as if she's about to be intimate. The she sighs and says in a very low tone, "When I wanted the job, we did some stuff, but I got the job and got to be really good friends with Tammy, and I was able to break it off with Emory."

"Sounds like Mr. Coogan is a pure asshole."

She laughs. "Not so pure."

Her drink arrives so she's quiet for a moment. "So, business is over? What's good here? I was flying high the last time I was here and can't remember."

"Classic Italian, even though Dan Tana was a...a Serb, I think."

She laughs. "So long as the food is good. If my geography is good that's just across the pond from Italy."

"You a meat-eater?"

"You bet, a real carnivore."'

"I know it's not the way things work nowadays, women's lib and all that stuff, but do you mind if I order?"

"Go for it, big boy."

I can't help but eye her up and down, but don't say that's exactly what I'm doing...going for it. We'll work that part out later.

I wave the waiter over. "A bottle of your best Malbec," I've already checked the menu and see I'm only risking seventy bucks, "A caprese salad to start, two fillets medium rare slathered in those great mushrooms, pasta putanesca on the side, and some asparagus."

And he's gone.

"How'd you know," she says, batting her eyes again, "that Malbec is my favorite?"

"You said you were a carnivore, so you gotta love the ultimate carnivore's red."

"I hope you're half as good at other things as you are at ordering." More eyelid bats.

"Ma'am, I aim to please."

"Then I'm going to skip dessert."

"You have an apartment nearby?"

"Yes, on the second floor of the same building I just came from. The company pays for it...but we can't go there." She cuts her eyes away and stares at the wall.

"Ah, because what's-his-face will be there. So you haven't exactly broken it off."

"Not totally," she says, and blushes a little, caught in a white lie.

"Where does he think you are?"

"Now you're embarrassing me."

"Where does he think you are?"

"Visiting my sister up in Valencia."

"Works for me. I'll bet the London up near Sunset has a room."

I don't normally get involved with involved women. But this one knows way more than she's telling, and if I'm going to find Tammy, I need to know everything. Every little intimate thing.

What a sacrifice a dutiful bodyguard has to make.

Target Shy & Sexy

Chapter Five

When we're halfway through our perfect steaks, she asks, "Tell me about Mike Reardon."

"Not much to tell. Born on the slopes of the Rockies, military for ten years or so, then out into the cold world."

"You're saving it? The world I mean. One of those guys?"

"Yeah, one miscreant at a time."

"You do more than bodyguard then?"

"I actually do very little in the bodyguard biz. I mostly do recovery work."

"So, like a car repossess guy?"

I have to laugh at that. "Yeah, if your car is worth a mil or so, otherwise I'll leave repo work to the real tough guys."

"So, you're not a tough guy?"

"Na, I'm a wuss. I only get angry with bullies, or wife beaters, or folks who steal their boss's yacht or airplane or retirement. And to be truthful, I hate dope dealers. But I normally call a cop."

"Why don't I believe that?"

"When you need a cop in seconds, he's only minutes away."

She laughs, then asks, "So, what's been your most exciting gig?"

"Can't tell, I'm sworn to silence. To be truthful, most of what I do folks don't want to talk about, or have their affairs talked about. I wouldn't have any new clients if I kiss and tell."

"You're not much of a conversationalist?"

"Now that hurts my feelings. Can't talk about work, but try me on literature, stage plays, movies, or the normal conversational clap trap."

"Okay, what's your favorite rock group?"

"The Eagles."

"You're older than you look."

"Again, you've hurt my feelings. I love classic rock. Who doesn't love living it up at the Hotel California?"

"Okay, you're classic, not old."

"Why does that sound like the same thing?"

She laughs. "If the shoe fits..." Then she adds, "You haven't asked about me."

"When I take on a job, I know more about all the players than they know about themselves."

"Oh, yeah. So, where did I go to college?"

"U.T., Austin, majored in Business, minored in music, got your B.A. but didn't finish your master's program as you got pregnant and daddy stopped with the funding. The boyfriend took a hike and you visited a clinic."

Her eyes widen and she glares at me, then her eyes soften. "Enough. Maybe I don't want to know what you know."

"I think you're a nice lady. We've all had our ups and downs. What I know about you is ninety-five percent good, and there's not many of us can say that."

We finish our cocktails, a bottle of wine, and a couple of after dinner drinks and I ask, "Did you drive or cab it here?"

"I cabbed it. I figured I might have a few drinks to drown my sorrows over my friend getting absconded with. So I cabbed it."

"You got a scarf?"

"Is the wind blowing? We gonna walk?"

"No, ma'am, you're gonna ride in style with the wind in your face."

"Then, let's go. I checked my jacket and can hold my hair down with it."

The Vette keeps my promise and she doesn't bother covering the hair. The windblown look is just fine on her. The London Hotel is a little high class for my normal overnight stays, but so's the lady, so I don't mind a bit.

The lady has a lovely body, makes all the right moves, but seems a little detached. She is no kicker, yeller or screamer. Nice, for recreational sex, but nothing to write home about, not that one writes home about such a thing. Of course, maybe there's some reticence on her part and I'm judging her unfairly. I do work up a sweat, so it's at least as good as a quick workout at the gym.

Even so the interlude was worth the bottle of good wine and great steak, and I did learn an interesting tidbit. It seems Emory

Coogan was on the verge of bankruptcy a few months ago and he tried to borrow money from Tammy Houston, and she told him no. Still, a month later, his fortunes must have turned, as he didn't file.

She leaves at midnight, saying that's how long it would have taken to visit her sister and drive back from Valencia.

I get a good night's sleep alone in a big king size bed, a light breakfast of juice and a bagel, then head out for Malibu. It's obvious Emory Coogan is not picking up my phone calls as all are going to the answering device. So it's time to get in his face.

As I'm going down the elevator I call Sol in Vegas and advise him of Coogan's former financial problems and get him on the prod.

And I presume the cop, Detective Howard Adamson, is at some regional sheriff's office. So I call him as soon as I get back on Sunset heading west. It turns out his office is in Agoura Hills, over the mountain near the Ventura Freeway. But he's heading for Malibu and we agree to meet for coffee.

We agree to meet at the Malibu Farm Pier Café, located at the foot of the pier. I can't imagine it's an easy spot to park near, but he picked it.

I'm a little surprised that for a mere ten bucks I can park in a lot just south of the pier. Who ever heard of an ocean front parking lot?

The place is a ramshackle old Spanish motif like a good part of Malibu, but what a location overlooking the pier and a nice stretch of white sand beach with enough bikini—even at mid-morning—to keep me interested. While I'm sipping my coffee and waiting, I get a text from Sol. Coogan borrowed a cool mil from Sammy Castiano, a contractor and road builder who also has a place on Dume Point, and gives me the address on Birdview. The plot thickens.

My coffee is cold and it's a little tough to get a warm up in a place that prides itself on the view, not the service, when Adamson finally wanders in.

He's looking a little better this mid-morning. No stains on the tie.

He plops across the table from me. "You buying, Reardon?"

"You bet, if you're candid about what you know."

"You're buying 'cause I can talk for the rest of the day and not tell you much."

I wave the waitress over. "Order up."

And he does, a full breakfast with a large orange juice.

I've worked up some appetite with my roll in the hay so I follow suit, and finally get my coffee warmed.

"So, any leads on who snatched our girl?" I ask.

"Not much. Our APB didn't pay off. The van obviously didn't stay on the Pacific Highway but there are a half-dozen ways to duck into the mountains and once you're over into Thousand Oaks or Agoura...or who knows, they could have holed up in the hills."

"No ransom note, no demands?"

"We've got two guys at the house with this Coogan guy, but nothing yet or I'd have heard."

"What do you know about a guy named Sammy Castiano?"

He eyes me for a moment, sipping his coffee, seeming to weigh his words. "You know Sammy Castiano from Vegas?"

"Never heard of the guy until this problem."

"He's got nothing to do with this."

"So, you know the guy?"

"Everybody around here knows, or knows of, Mr. Castiano. Big name in Malibu. Hell, big name in California. Road builder, heavy Democrat contributor. Had a fund raiser for the president last year with fifty of the biggest names in Hollywood in his backyard. I took time off to work security for him. He pays big and in cash. What's Castiano have to do with this?"

"Probably nothing…but I have reason to believe Coogan borrowed some major dough from him a year or so ago."

"Hell, that doesn't mean a thing—"

"Unless this Castiano is mobbed up."

Adamson laughs out loud. Then shakes his head. "Just because his name ends in a vowel."

I don't break a smile, in fact I bore in. "Is he mobbed up?"

He sobers a little, and glares at me, but he has a twitch in one eye. Were we playing poker I'd think that a tell.

"How the hell would I know?" he snaps a little too energetically. "We've got an organized crime unit but they work out of Monterey Park. As far as I know Mr. Castiano is a solid citizen."

We're cordial enough as we finish our breakfast, but after the tab comes and the girl takes my card, he lays one on me.

"Reardon. You don't have the best rep, and you don't have any brass worth flashing here in California…nothing that means squat. I pulled a sheet on you and you got no wants or warrants, however, you know that concealed carry permit you have from Wyoming is good for anything but butt wipe here in California. You carrying now?"

"If I were, and since I have no right to do so, do you think I'd mention it?"

"No, you wouldn't mention it, but I just asked."

"I guess it's your right to ask."

"How about I shake you down right now?"

"You ever hear of probable cause, Detective?"

"Yeah. And I think just you being you is probable cause."

It's my turn to laugh. "Maybe I should be complimented?"

"Maybe you should stand up and put your hands on the table, feet back."

"Maybe you should go fuck yourself."

We stare at each other for a moment, then he shrugs, then adds, "Don't get in the way of my investigation."

"Detective, we were doing fine until I mentioned Castiano. He your brother-in-law or what?"

He stammers a little, "He's an upstanding citizen who supports lots of good causes. You stay away from Sammy."

"Sammy?"

"Yes, Sammy Castiano. Or I won't worry about any probable cause."

I rise and head for the door, waving over my shoulder. "I'll let you know if I turn anything up."

He shouts after me. "You stay the fuck out of my case."

"You're welcome for the breakfast."

He gives me the middle finger.

There are only a half-dozen other patrons, but all stare at Adamson, who's getting red in the face as I stop at the register and sign my ticket. I give the waitress a wink. "Don't mind my friend. He's a cop and thinks he can talk that way in front of anyone." She glares at him then looks at the tip and smiles as I head for the parking lot.

Now to get in Coogan's face.

Target Shy & Sexy

Chapter Six

Anew player.

This guy is even bigger than Butch Horrigan and looks to be about five percent body fat. However, he's a gym rat with biceps, triceps, traps and lats so big he probably has to call for help to wipe his butt. If muscle bound were in the dictionary his picture would be the example. I park the Vette at the end of the walk as if I pulled in the driveway he might, just might, be able to turn it over and that would piss me off.

He places his book down and wanders off the covered porch where he's parked in a swinging love seat. All that beef and reading a book.

I move around the car to meet him.

"Quantum theory or what?" I ask.

"Uhh…" he mumbles.

"That's what I thought. Comic book?"

"You mean what was I reading?"

"You win."

"Nothing."

He's carrying the book so I reach down and turn his wrist so I can see the cover. It's a gay novel by the picture on the cover.

"Hey," he grumbles, and jerks back.

"I'll bet you're Lance or Bruce?"

"I'm Harry."

I can't pass that up. "Bullshit, I bet you shave every square inch of that well-oiled bod of yours."

"Who are you, Mr. Curious, and what's your business?"

"Is Mr. Coogan home? I'm here to reset the thermostats." I'm wishing I had my van with one of the many magnetic signs I carry, Thompson Heating and Ventilating, but I don't. He'd probably buy it if I did.

"Bullshit. You in that old Corvette."

"That happens to be a cherry '57 with the original paint and upholstery."

"Still old."

"Okay, you're pissing me off now. Get Coogan for me before I shove that paperback up your butt…come to think of it you're wishing I would, aren't you, Handsome Harry?"

He drops the book on the flagstone walkway and takes a hint of a defensive posture. He's probably got a belt in karate and thinks he's indestructible. False security. He growls. "Coogan is busy. Leave your card in the mailbox and I'll tell him you stopped by."

"Against the law."

"What?" he asks, looking a little perplexed.

"A federal crime."

"What the fuck are you talking about?"

"You can't put anything but mail in a mail box. Any imbecile knows that."

He's beginning to turn a little red. But I comply and pull a Mike Reardon Repairman card out of my wallet. I fold it in half longways and step forward, acting as if I'm going to hand it to him. "We don't want to go to the federal slammer, now do we?"

I keep the card six inches from my chest until I'm within arm's length of him, then lash out and poke him in the eye with it.

"Yeooow," he yells, and grabs his eye and does a little two step, which gives me the opportunity to do a sweep with my left foot, knocking his out from under him. He goes down hard, as a guy over two-forty would, and hits hard enough on his right shoulder that I'm surprised the flagstone doesn't crack. He oofs, grabs his right shoulder with his left hand and rolls away, then rocks back and forth like his shoulder is separated. I doubt it. But he has an automatic in a hard-plastic holster on his right hip and I reach down and pop it free, pop and pocket the clip, and eject the chamber shell into the flowers. Then I drop it on the flagstone.

I move away and over to a driveway, which is fenced from the rear, and to a four-car garage by a swinging car width gate. But there's a lower human pass-through gate on the side next to the house. The swinging car gate is at least six feet high, the pass-through is only five. I guess the great security mind that designed the place thinks a car can jump higher than a person? I give them a lesson and vault the pass through person gate. Circling to the back, with the beautiful view of the Pacific beyond, a bevy of gulls circling overhead, and a beached whale on a double-wide chaise lounge next to the pool—Emory Coogan, obscene in a speedo lost in the cracks of fat.

"What the fuck?" he manages as I walk over and plop my butt down on the adjoining chaise.

"I need a little information."

He's trying to rise up but I push him back down, making him spill some drink with an umbrella in it.

"Coogan, is that how you get your juice in the morning?"

"It's damn near noon. Not that it's any of your business. What information?"

"I'm working on the case of the missing country singer, you know, Tammy Houston."

"Not on our dollar you ain't." He again tries to sit up and I again shove him down. He continues, "You prick, you let me up and I'll stomp your butt."

"I'm tempted, but I don't have time. What's your deal with Sammy Castiano?"

He eyes me carefully. "Never heard of the fucker."

"I think I will let you up," and I push the chaise I'm on back and rise. "Can I give you a hand, fat man?"

I extend my left to his right and help pull him to his feet and he comes up with a round house left that I slough off, then slap him hard with my right palm. Then backhand him, then give him the palm again and I know his ears are ringing and his eyes spinning. Just as I finish the last slap, I see Harry the Hairless round the corner at a run, his automatic in hand.

I can see he hasn't bothered to check to see if the clip's in place and it's not, so I'm not too concerned. I shove the fat man and he windmills his arms and lands flat on his back in the deep end of the pool with a splash to rival a broaching whale.

Harry charges to within three feet of me—the dumb shit—and lays down on me with the auto. "I'm gonna fuck you up," he says, as I step into him.

I turn the auto into him, inside, then over with the wrist as he's compressing the trigger and getting no bang for his buck. He goes to his back and I continue to twist the wrist and step over as he goes over to his stomach, yelling loud enough that the gulls seem a lullaby. Then, just for the hell of it, I kick him hard on the twisted arm just above the shoulder joint, and now I know his shoulder is, this time, truly separated. He's out of the game for about six weeks. I pick up the weapon and toss it into the deep end of the pool so as not to give him any more false security.

Emory is trying to lift himself out of the pool without benefit of the ladder and I move over and put a foot on his shoulder and shove him back down, and under. He comes up spitting.

I stand beside the pool until he tries to get out again, and again shove him under. He comes up again, this time a little red in the face and spitting even more.

"I should just drown both of your dumb asses, but I'll settle for an answer to my question."

Emory spits and chokes, then manages, "What question?"

"What's your deal with Sammy Castiano?"

"He's kind of a neighbor, lives around the point. I got no deal with him."

"Who has Tammy?"

"I wish I knew." He glances over at Harry, who's now sitting up rubbing his shoulder and looking like he might break out in tears any second. "Did you break his arm?" Then when I don't answer, he yells at Harry. "Hey, you worthless fuck. I thought you were a bodyguard."

"Yeah," I answer, "he trained at the same school Butch Horrigan did."

I start to move away, then turn back to Coogan. "Hey, fat man, I'm gonna do the job Tammy hired me to do, and it looks to me like you are right in the middle of this deal and part of the problem, not the solution. If she comes home in anything but one piece, I'm gonna rip you apart a pound of suet at a time. You got that?"

"Get the fuck off this property."

So I do, this time I don't have to vault the pass though gate as there's a latch low on the inside. I'm not surprised to see Detective Howard Adamson's car pulling up behind mine. He is out of it by the time I'm there.

"I thought you were told to stay away from here?" he snaps.

"No, no, you got it all wrong. I was invited to the pool party. Didn't I mention it at breakfast?"

"I told you to stay away from my case."

"Purely a social visit, Detective. Wanted to see how Tammy's grieving associates were getting along."

As I'm getting behind the wheel of the Vette, he's shouting after me, "Stay out of my case, Reardon."

I wave over my shoulder as I peel out.

I'm not going far, as it's only a half-mile around the point to Sammy Castiano's place.

Chapter Seven

A h, anyone who may end up creeping a place has got to love Google Earth.

I park a block away and pull up the aerial of the Castiano compound, and I say compound as there's more than one house. Probably the smaller is a guesthouse, then a garage to contain at least six vehicles, one door large enough for one of those million-dollar motor homes. There's a greenhouse that's at least forty by one hundred feet beyond the garage and what must be a gardener's shack attached thereto. A small cottage and gatehouse is only thirty feet back from the road and the driveway makes a wide circle from the gatehouse to a porte cochere in front of the main house that would cover four limos, then on to the garages, then a slight stubby driveway leads off to the side to a two-car garage attached to the guest house. The whole thing is a sort of Greco Italian Renaissance with a little Mediterranean thrown in. Arches, red tile roofs, but lots of glass. It's two stories tall over most of the main house. It must be a hundred yards from the rear of the house to the ocean with a cliff of forty or fifty feet. Google Earth shows me a small structure cliff side with a fair size deck cantilevered out over crashing surf below.

Between house and cliff house is a pool large enough to float a fair size yacht and two short golf holes with their own greens, plus a putting green. I can make out what must be pads for driving balls out into the sea, a rich man's version of a driving range.

The landscaping is mostly old eucalypti with a few wind-blown Monterey pines rising out of enough shrubs to make a real fire hazard. However the place is far enough from the Malibu Hills to not have to worry much. Some gardener has a full time job as there's color everywhere.

It's a hell of a place. But not for the sake of security. Unless there are a couple of Rottweilers, I can get window side on the main house without ever being spotted.

But I decide to try the direct route first.

I pull into the driveway and stop at the gatehouse. I expected a no-neck goomba who looked to be right out of Detroit, and am a little surprised to see a pencil neck who sounds like he's right out of a Donald Duck cartoon. And he's got the tight lips and no chin. He fully fills the bill, so to speak.

"Hi, I'm Richard Strong, here to see Mr. Castiano."

"You have an appointment?" he quacks.

"This is April 4th?"

"Yes, sir."

"Then I have an appointment."

"I don't have you on the calendar and I'm afraid Mr. Castiano is in town. Are you sure it wasn't with Mrs. Castiano?"

I do a quick brain search and remember Sol's report. "Margo...well, he said maybe he and Margo. But just Margo would be fine."

"Your name again?"

"Strong. Richard Strong...friends call me Dick."

He doesn't bat an eye but rather picks up the phone and hits a button or two.

"Yes, ma'am." He says, and I can see he's working a device like a game console and a small video camera on the edge of the building pans the car then stops, aimed directly at my face. I can see Donald Duck eying a monitor, and see my own smiling mug increasing in size thereon as he zooms in. He still has the receiver to his ear.

"Yes, ma'am," he says, with a nod of the head, then turns to me.

"Someone will meet you at the door and show you in."

I smile and drive away, resisting the urge to say "Thanks, Daffy."

As I park under the porte cochere, a door befitting the Halls of Congress opens and a guy in black pants and coat but sans tie and with the top three buttons of the shirt undone, strolls out and walks around the Vette to where I'm climbing out. He's got a bit of an early Frank Sinatra look about him, not over five-foot-eight and a buck fifty. He doesn't extend a hand, but nods.

"I'm Tony, I take care of the house and grounds. You're Mr. Strong."

"That's me, Tony. Nice job on the house and grounds, pardner."

"Thanks. I have a little help with it all."

"I imagine."

"Mrs. Castiano is out by the pool if you'll follow me, please."

He starts to lead the way, then we're both stopped by a loud, "Wow!" and I glance to the doorway where a tall, and I imagine formerly gorgeous blonde, is standing in a pool wrap, high heels, a sun hat as big as an umbrella, and quite a bit of skin showing around a way too itty bitty yellow polka dot bikini. She charges forward and spreads her arms wide, not at me, but at the Vette.

"Do you have the provenance on this beauty? I had one brand new in '57 when I was just sixteen."

As she nears I can see she's had one too many facelifts and has the telltale frog mouth, her eyes beginning to look a little Oriental.

"No, ma'am. I bought her in Vegas less than ten years ago, from some guy who rolled the bones one time too often."

She walks up and down the car, teetering a little on the five inch heels. This gal has got to be in her seventies, but she's pretty amazing to still be in the bikini. The skin on her hands, arms, and lower legs gives away her age a little, but all and all she's amazing.

She turns, and the slightly faded blue eyes narrow a little. "You tired of her yet? Wanna sell her?"

"No, she's part of the family now. But I'm complimented you asked."

"Come on in. It's not quite noon but I'll make an exception for a guy who has a beautiful cherry fifty-seven. Tony, pop a bottle of the good stuff."

"Yes, ma'am," Tony says from behind me as I have to stride out to keep up with Margo. Champagne, which I imagine is the good stuff, is a lot better than crawling through the underbrush to creep the place. I should try this technique more often.

She throws off her net wrap and steps into the Jacuzzi. "Peel down, Angelo. We're not bashful around here."

"Uh...I'm not Angelo, Mrs. Castiano."

Her eyes widen a little. "You're not the decorator?"

"No, ma'am. I actually came to have a chat with Mr. Castiano."

"Well, bless your black little heart. You wandered right in here like you were somebody. I thought you looked way too straight to be Angelo."

I have to laugh, then add, "I'm Dick Strong, over from Vegas, working on the abduction of one of your neighbors."

"You a cop or something?" She seems to relax a little and sinks on down into the hot water.

"Something. I do recovery work, including missing folks upon occasion."

"A private dick?"

"No, ma'am—"

"Will you quit with the fuckin' ma'am. I'm Mrs. Castiano or Margo."

"Yes, ma'am...I mean, thanks, Margo. And no, not a private dick. I do carry a bail enforcement badge and sometimes do a little of that work."

"Bounty hunter?"

"Yep, upon occasion, but mostly recovery work."

"Sounds like muscle work to me...you're built for it."

"Thanks. But I try to use the brain when possible."

"You might as well peel down and jump in. At least I'll know if you've got any weapons on you," then she laughs, and adds, "or a decent weapon."

She's still giggling when Tony shows up with a tray in professional waiter fashion carrying with one hand a bottle of fancy champagne, two flutes, and a small bowl of chocolates.

"You coming in?"

"No, thanks. No time to display my weapons, but I'll have a glass with you before I have to run."

She feigns a pout, then laughs, "So, you gonna haul my old man to the slammer?"

"Nope, no contract on Mr. Castiano."

"You and a dozen others like you couldn't do it anyway. So, what's up?"

Tony has poured and handed me a flute. Before I answer, I take a sip. "Wow, that's good stuff."

"Ought to be at two hundred a bottle."

"True. What's up is I'm looking for info on the abduction of Tammy Houston."

"What's that got to do with us?"

"Came to me on the grapevine that Mr. Çastiano loaned Tammy's manager a large chunk of dough."

She shrugs. "Hell, Sammy loans lots of folks money."

I smile tightly. "Folks who disappear when they don't pay back."

Her smile fades, and her eyes shoot daggers, then with a tight jaw, she yells, "Tony. The gentleman is leaving."

"Thanks for the sip, and the presumption," I say, and place the flute back on the tray.

"Presumption?"

"Yeah, that I'm a gentleman."

Tony appears in the doorway, and suddenly behind him are two no-necks, nicely dressed, but still goomba boys. And they are not smiling.

Tony takes a few steps forward and notes the scowl on Margo's remodeled face, then asks, "You want him tossed, or just shown out?"

Target Shy & Sexy

Chapter Eight

I answer for him. "Only three of you, or you got another half-dozen hid out somewhere?"

"You don't think three of us are up to tossing you?"

"Nope."

"Margo?" he asks.

Again, she's smiling. "I think Sergio can take him without any help."

"He's the curly haired one, I'll bet," I say.

"You got it," she says, then giggles a little crazily.

The two others are filling the six-foot width of the open side of a sliding glass door leading out to the patio. The taller but thinner of the two steps aside and gives a head bow to Sergio, who grins broadly.

I'm glad I didn't get all dressed up this morning. Hiking boots, jeans, and a pullover. I customarily wear a heavy belt buckle, and have a wide belt and eight ounces of buckle on, but even though it's a good weapon I won't need it with only one guy to deal with.

Sergio is two inches shorter, at an even six feet, but weighs about the same. He's been a muscle fuck at some earlier time in his life, but has gone to a nice suet overlay. His six-pack is hidden under a hundred six packs of Lucky Lager. His nose has been broken more than once, he's got crisscrossed scars in both eyebrows, and one ear is cauliflowered. Wrestler, I'll bet. And no virgin to street fighting after his wrestling career was over. If so, I'll fool him as I wrestled in college and know most the moves and have invented a couple of new ones.

Obviously I didn't make much of an impression on Margo if she thinks this guy is gonna toss me.

"Hold on," I say, and Margo and the rest of them begin to laugh. "I don't mean hold up on the contest, I just thought y'all would like to cover this." I snatch my wallet from my back pocket and pop a Franklin out and lay it nicely on a glass top table. "Odds?"

Margo gets a curious look. "You want to bet a hundred Sergio won't take you, and you want odds?"

"Y'all are pretty confident that the Italian Stallion here will put me away, so yeah, I want odds. This pretty boy is probably the heavyweight champ of Italy."

Margo laughs. "How about five to one."

I smile tightly. "That'll make it worth my while."

"Tony, my purse," she says, and Tony hustles inside.

Sergio stretches his eighteen-inch biceps wide, and yawns. He doesn't seem worried in the least. Tony is back in a heartbeat and hands Margo her wallet. She peels out five fresh Franklins and literally covers mine with hers.

"Sergio, I'm tiring of this," she says, and gives him a bit of a disgusted look.

I move a couple of steps away from the Jacuzzi, and Sergio charges. He fakes his hands upward, then dives in low for a double leg takedown…as I suspected, a wrestler. I post off his head with my left hand, kick my legs back putting all my weight on the head, and drive his face into the flagstone, then pivot around to his back while he's trying to clear the cobwebs. Like any good wrestler he tries to get his knees under him so he can sit out and spin into me, but I have a hand on the wrist of the hand he's using to rise up, and, drive my head into his armpit and wrench the wrist back and up into a hammer lock. He continues his sit out and I wrench the elbow back and feel his shoulder go. So I let go, knowing he's finished even if he doesn't. He spins away and gets to his feet, but his left hand is on his shoulder and his eyes are tearing—sweet Sergio may just yell for his mama. Nothing hurts much more than a separated shoulder.

Then the fool charges me, and I'm sure can barely see as his eyes are watering so badly, and I sidestep—and he joins Margo in the Jacuzzi, graceful as a hippo, splashing her coif with a wave that inundates the large blonde doo, and it goes straight in an instant and I'm surprised to see, cants to the side. A wig.

"Damn you, Sergio. You've ruined my hair!"

No neck number two is having none of it and charges throwing a roundhouse as he does, as I spin to the side sloughing off the punch and stomp down on his knee as he passes. It crumples and he rides it to the flagstone, screaming in an embarrassing falsetto—one leg out in front, one strangely bent to the side.

I turn back to the Jacuzzi and the cursing woman.

"Mrs. Castiano, you're in about ten grand in medical bills so far. Wanna go for twenty?"

Sergio is spitting and hacking, trying to clear the water out of his lungs while rubbing his shoulder. Mrs. Castiano's mouth is puckered so tightly you couldn't drive a sixteen penny nail in with a sledge, and her red face shows even through the pancake makeup. No neck two is rolling around on the flagstone, holding his knee in both hands and moaning in a low tone, way more manly than the falsetto.

"You fucker," Margo manages. "Tony, where are you Tony?"

With a side-glance I'd caught Tony disappearing through the sliding glass door, and that concerned me. And I was right as he's roaring back through the doorway, a large semi-auto pistol in hand.

I drag the little .380 from the small of my back where it was stowed under my pull over, drop to one knee where Margo is directly behind me, and have the weapon centered on the center of Tony's chest.

"Margo," I snap, without turning back to her. "You're about to add the cost of a funeral to your already high medical bills."

"Tony!" she screams, "You're the best houseboy we ever had. Put that down before dipshit here lays you out or you hit me."

Tony skids to a stop. It's a green Ruger SR9 he's carrying and I can see by the pop-up on the top that it's not cocked.

"Tony," I say with a little condemnation in my voice, "you better leave the grunt work to the goomba boys here. Even though I'm sure they're not good at it either. Your weapon is <u>not</u> cocked, and if you cock it I'm going to blow your cock off."

He's turning red in the face and doing a little dance like a nervous hen about to lay an egg.

"Tony," Margo yells again. "Put the piece down."

And he does, but I can see the whole thing frustrates him a lot. I walk to the little glass top table and pick up the six hundred. Maybe the total of what I'll make for this whole gig, then head for the door. As I come even with Tony, I pause to use the Ruger for a hockey puck and put it in the nearby deep end of the swimming pool with a nice side-kick, then keep walking.

I slip into the Vette, fire her up and am pulling away when I see two other Castiano employees are in the main garage, one vacuuming and one polishing a van...a white van, as was described at the scene of Tammy's abduction.

Target Shy & Sexy

Chapter Nine

I love it when I tangle and don't bust a knuckle, and I didn't. Not even a bruise.

One of the great things about the 21st Century is satellite radio, and I'm in a good mood and feeling a little like an outlaw, so I tune in Outlaw Country and get in the middle of I'm The Only Hell My Mama Ever Raised and Johnny Paycheck is doing a great job as always. I'm trying to remember the words and sing along as I pull out onto Pacific Coast Highway, and don't get through one verse before red and blue lights fill my rear view mirrors. Luckily we're in one of the few spots in Malibu where one can easily pull over, and I do. I slip the .380 out of its holster shoved in my belt at the small of my back, pop the clip, and leave the little Smith and Wesson on the passenger seat. I also work the slide and eject the one in the chamber.

I'm only a little surprised when the CHP opens his white door with the huge badge emblazoned thereon, and crouches behind it, weapon drawn. He looks like a surfer dude in uniform, blonde hair shining in the sun.

"Keep the hands where I can see them. Climb out, hands on your head, and back this way."

I do, and to his credit, he tells me to lean over the back of the Vette. "Just hold there for a minute."

I hear another car slide to a stop behind him, and footsteps trotting our way.

"My back up has you covered, hot shot." He pats me down, a good job including crotch and ankles. "I'm gonna hook you up so leave your left hand on your head and place your right hand behind your back." He does. "Now your left." He keeps a hand between my shoulder blades, with pressure forward, keeping me off balance over the trunk of the Vette.

Good police procedure on their part. I'm impressed.

"Anything in your pockets I should worry about? Needle maybe?"

"No, sir. Live it up."

He digs my wallet out and flips it open. "Michael Reardon. The name phone-in was Dick Strong."

"That's a condition, not a name."

"Very funny."

"So, you got the wrong guy. How about cutting me loose?"

"FFC," he says.

"Fat fucking chance."

"California Highway Patrol officers don't swear...at least not on the job."

"Admirable," I offer.

"You want him?" the highway patrolman asks the other officer, who I now see is an L.A. County Sheriff.

"Yes, I got a call from one of our detectives, right after I saw the APB, and he definitely wants him."

"My pleasure," the CHP says.

"And we were getting on so well," I say to the blonde surfer cop, and flash him a grin, his nameplate says Brown. "The surf's up and you having to work. A real pity. So, did uncle Moonbeam get you the job?" I'd ruin my well-established rep if I wasn't a little bit of a smart ass. Brown ignores me.

"I've got to wait for another unit and a tow truck," the sheriff says, and I see by his nameplate, he's De La Hoya. He's light for a Hispanic.

"De La Hoya, there's a weapon on the passenger seat. Please note it's unloaded and in plain sight. And make it a trailer, not a tow truck. You're on notice that the car is a classic antique and worth about fifty grand."

"Oh, yeah," he says. "You got a permit to carry?"

"I do. A Wyoming permit."

He laughs. We both know California doesn't recognize permits from any other state, and consequently many other states don't recognize California's.

"What's the charge?" I ask, maybe a little too adamantly. "I wasn't speeding."

"Ha, that's hardly the charge. Home invasion."

I have to chuckle at that one. "So, I invaded a home by myself, a home with five or six armed goomba guards right out of the Godfather and one Mafia mama who thinks she's a blonde Sophia Loren...and is about the same age?"

"That's the call we got."

I laugh again, then add, "And you believe and double down on any call coming from the Castiano compound?"

"Not your concern. Move back to my unit on the passenger side. You're going in the back seat to wait."

He's got a hand on my elbow and again with good cop procedure keeps pressure on it, throwing me off balance just enough to rob confidence.

"You related to Oscar?" I ask.

"Not that I know of. You a fan?"

"Damn right. Hard not to be."

"If he shows up at a family reunion, I'll give him your regards." He opens the back door and with a hand on my head and one on my elbow, ushers me in.

"Careful with the Vette," I admonish as he slams the door.

So, I'm off to the lockup, about my twentieth time.

I wish I was as zoned out as my buddy Pax, so I could use up the waiting time with a nap. Not to be. Instead, I pass the time listening to the cop calls until another unit arrives and they toss the car, bag the weapon, and the tow truck arrives. De La Hoya has paid little attention to my admonitions as it's a Tommy's Towing Truck, the conventional variety.

Why am I not surprised when we arrive at the L. A. County Sheriff's station, in Agoura, over the Santa Monica Mountains near the Ventura freeway, and I'm ushered into a conference room to be greeted by my favorite dick. Frumpy as always, potbelly straining at his shirt buttons, however there are no stains on his tie...yet. He's sipping coffee white with cream, so hope reigns eternal.

De La Hoya hooks me to an iron loop on the table top, so at least my arms are in front and I can lean on my elbow.

"How you doin', Howard?" I say, and De La Hoya gives me a curious look, then slips out.

"You screwed up my lunch hour."

"Sorry about that. How about you going back to lunch and I'll head for the impound to pick up my Vette?"

"I doubt if you'll see your little ride for a couple of years. If not a lot more if they can make the home invasion stick."

I have to chuckle.

"You think that's amusing?" he asks.

"I do, and so do you. If this guy wasn't a major Moonbeam supporter, you'd be giving me a pat on the head for bringing his help down to size."

"A little more than that. You busted one's leg."

"Yeah, and mussed Margo's wig and embarrassed her main man, Sergio. Big fucking deal."

"What the hell were you doing there?" he asks.

"Enjoying the seaside. You told me to stay away from your case."

"What the hell were you doing there?"

"I guess you didn't notice a white van was one of the vehicles in the garage."

"There are lots of white vans in California. A couple of hundred thousand, or more, I'd guess."

"Right on, however not owned by someone who's owed a mil or more by Tammy Houston's manager."

"Man, that's a stretch."

I hear the door open behind me, and Howard jumps to his feet.

"Leave us, Howard. Bring me a coffee." It's a deep raspy voice. Harold heads around one side of the table, and a guy in a three thousand dollar gray sharkskin suit that had to be tailored by Omar the tent maker, circles the other side and plops down in the seat Harold formerly occupied. He's a very fat man, with a small inner tube for a neck and another set of bulges under his ears. The white shirt has to be tailored as well, but the collar button is open and the blue and gray striped tie pulled down three inches. A puff of gray chest hair shows above the knot. He's not bald, but there's a cul-de-sac on the top of his head all the way back and encompassing his pate. The hair he has is gray and trimmed to a quarter inch. And he has a Hollywood stylish four or five days of whisker growth, gray matching his hair.

He puts both fat elbows on the table and steeples his corncob size fingers alongside his wide nose, dividing watery gray eyes. He gives me a knowing look, then shakes his head.

"You gonna owe me a few grand, tough guy."

We're both silent as Harold returns with a cup of coffee. He forgot mine.

"Where's your manners, Harold?" I snap, and he waves a center finger at me as he leaves.

So I turn back to the fat man. "I presume you're Castiano?" No reply, like everyone should know, so I continue. "A few grand? For taking advantage of your hospitality, or what?"

"It's mister to you. A few grand for fucking up my second cousin, Sergio and his dipshit buddy who I should never have hired. And for scaring my houseboy half to death. Tony's a nice boy. And you really pissed Margo off. She's five grand apiece into those wigs."

"So, consider it a test run on your security and the quality of Margo's hair piece. Where do I send the bill?"

Target Shy & Sexy

Chapter Ten

Y ou're a real wise ass," Castiano says.

"Just doing my job."

"Which is?"

"Finding Tammy Houston."

He shrugs. "Ain't my problem."

"Oh, I think it is."

"Why's that?"

"Coogan owes you a cool mil—"

"Mil two, with the vig."

"Whatever. Tammy's guy, who depends upon Tammy for every dime he makes, owes you dough."

"Dumb fuck shouldn't like the tables so much."

"And Tammy was hit by some guys in a white van...and guess what the Castiano garage holds?"

"What?"

"A white van."

He laughs, kind of a low rumble that comes up from somewhere in his voluminous body. "And you think I'd be so stupid to use my own vehicle? What with CSI like it is these days. Don't you watch T.V., Reardon?"

"What's to gain by snatching Tammy? Isn't that kind of like killing the goose that laid the golden egg?"

"I like the girl and I think she likes me just fine. She's been to a couple of functions at my place and even went with Margo shopping. She's like family."

"Yeah, and you'd sell your grandma for a quarter."

He gets red in the face. "Look, you smartass punk, I take care of family and you don't even think about mentioning my people. Everybody thinks that because I live on the water and do okay, that I don't have anyone to answer to. We all got people to answer to. I got an eight figure payback coming up, and I got to have that dough back from that Irish piece of shit."

I shrug. The grandma remark was probably uncalled for.

His tone levels out a little. "You haven't ask me if I'm gonna press charges."

"The home invasion is a hoot. Who'd buy that? You might get me on simple assault, but even a first year law student could probably get me off on that one. Three guys and poor little me. And I bet Sergio and the dipshit have sheets as long as my arm—"

"Yours ain't exactly a piece of note paper."

"—and no, you're not gonna press charges. It's not your style. Blindside me in an alley, maybe. You really are not interested in being embarrassed...a tough guy like you...with having one guy wander in and fuck up your muscle. Hell, everyone will be doing it if they think it's that easy."

He's silent for a moment, then eyes me with his pig eyes. "Tell you what, smart guy. You beat a trail back to Wyoming, or wherever friggin' hillbilly place you hail from, and I'll forget the whole thing." He looks up at the video camera on a ceiling-high mount and holds a fat hand up so his lips can't be seen. His whisper is more like a rasp. "Otherwise, next time it's both knees, and the third time if you're dumb enough to come back in a year or so when you heal up. That will be the charm. Chum for my shark fishing."

I shrug. No sense in intimidating him more than I already have. After all. Governor Moonbeam does come to his house for fundraisers.

He gets up and strides around the table, amazingly light on his feet for a fat guy who must be in his seventies, and the door closes behind me then almost as quickly opens again.

Harold rounds the table and takes his seat again.

I give him my best boy scout smile. "You cutting me loose?"

"Nope."

"How about my phone call?"

"As soon as you're processed."

"You know that guy in Peanuts...the one with the flies always circling his head."

"What are you talking about?"

"I'm pretty sure he was your namesake." His tie is now spotted, coffee with cream, I imagine.

"Fuck you, Reardon."

"Uncuff me and I'll take bets about who's the fuckee."

He rises and goes back to the door, and yells out. "Parkenson, back me up here."

A big burly black sergeant fills the doorway as Harold uncuffs me from the table tie-down, then re-cuffs me behind my back.

"Process him in," Harold says.

"What charge?" the sergeant asks.

"Stupidity. How about a seventy-two hour psychiatric hold." He guffaws as if he's enjoyed his own joke, then adds, "No, felony assault will do for the time being."

"My phone call?" I ask, but Harold is walking away, so I turn to the sergeant who's now guiding me down the hall with a ham-like hand on my upper arm. "My phone call?"

"Soon as you're processed," he says.

"Thanks."

And he's a man of his word. I have to call Pax collect.

"Wondered where you've been?" he asks.

"Lounging, at the expense of the County of Los Angeles."

"Enjoying yourself and the accommodations? How much bail money?"

"I don't know, call Mort downtown and get him on it, and," I hesitate as I'm sure I'm being recorded, then figure, what the hell, "and get someone on properties owned by Sammy...Samuel probably...Castiano, et. al., et. ex., partnerships, corporations...the whole bit. As soon as I'm out of here I'll want to meet someone at Barstow and trade vehicles. I'll need my..." again I hesitate, "...my work rig."

"You need some backup?"

"I may, but I'll let you know."

"What's up with the girl?"

"Not much more, but I'm getting pissed so I'll be hitting it lots harder."

"What's the charge?"

"Felony assault, but it's totally hokey."

"What?"

"I beat up a couple of guys and screwed up the hairdo of an old broad."

"Old guys?" He laughs.

"Just give Mort a call, please."

"Will do."

They throw me in the drunk tank. I look good in jail orange and flip-flops. The good news, it isn't Saturday night so the place is not so puke covered as it might be. The better news, it isn't downtown so of the six drunks in the twenty-foot square cell, four of them are in business suits. I find a bench and plop down, and am soon sawing logs. I guess I've missed lunch so the next time I open my eyes, we're being led out to supper. Jail food ain't what it used to be. Now you actually get some healthy stuff with your white bread, pasta, beans, or potatoes. I'm not returned to the drunk tank, but rather to a cell with three black-ink tat-covered Hispanic guys who are about my age and look fresh from the cartel and the border. I'm motioned to a top bunk and take it without arguing.

The boys eye me up and down but say nothing until I light in the upper bunk. Then one who looks a little like El Gordo the Mexican professional wrestler, leans on my bunk and asks, "Hey, pendejo, you suck cocks?"

"Why, you a pussy maricon?" I ask if he's queer.

He growls and I sit up enough so I have a leg cocked and can drive one of my flip-flops down his throat if he reaches for me.

I'm surprised to see he has the globe and anchor tat on his neck, so I add. "Semper Fi."

He gets a half-assed grin, gives me a thumbs up, then backs away and sits in a blackjack game with his two buddies.

I'd like to say I slept well, but one eye open is not very restful.

I get two more meals on the county before a jailer comes for me in the middle of the afternoon. "Roll it up, Reardon. You're bailed."

The officer on the desk hands me a card, which shouldn't be a surprise as Tammy's abduction will be considered a kidnapping, and a high profile one. The card is FBI Special Agent Robbie Quintana. And I'm instructed to call her. I pick up my stuff and change clothes, happy to return the jail orange, and when I exit a side door into the parking lot, am very surprised to see a tall brunette leaning on a new Mercedes.

"Hi, Reardon. You don't write, you don't call. This is a hell of a way to have to meet up."

"Tyler Thompson, as I live and breathe...."

Chapter Eleven

And I'm glad you still do," she says, then adds, "Live and breathe, I mean. I'm a little surprised as I hear you stormed the ramparts at the Castiano place." She sighs deeply, then asks, "Is it too early for a cocktail?"

"Only if the joint has a shower. I smell like a feed yard and feel like I need to be run through a truck wash. You haven't seen anyone else here to bail me?"

"Nope. Somebody called while I was doing the paperwork." She flashes a smile and look that would melt a weaker man, then adds, "Well, big boy, there's a Hampton Inn just down the road and about a half mile from it is the Thousand Oaks version of The Grill On The Alley. Probably not as good as jail food. I'll loan you enough dough to buy dinner."

"Unless they stole my credit cards, I can handle it. Any idea where they might have impounded my wheels?"

"It's in your release docs, I'll bet. Odds are it's back in Malibu. How about that shower...I'll even climb in with you and scrub your back. Then we go to the Grill; then we worry about your precious Vette."

"What do I owe you for bail?"

"Ten grand."

"What?"

"Ten grand. I paid all cash. No bondsman."

"Good, then you'll get it all back, and I'll pay a handsome rate of interest in the meantime."

"You bet you will, starting right after that shower."

I give her a closer look. "Is that makeup over a black eye?"

"It doesn't matter."

"It matters to me. That fucking Coogan?"

"It was an accident. He was a little pissed when he called my sister's and found out I hadn't been there and was just swinging his arms. He's clumsy as hell."

"Yeah, so clumsy he's going to fall down and bust all his front teeth out."

"Let's go shower up."

"Swing into the Thousand Oaks Mall and Macy's. I need some clean clothes."

"How about Nordstrom's?"

"You hit Nordstrom's while I hit Macy's."

"No, you need an overseer. Besides, my closet is full of Nordstrom's."

"Nothing new about Tammy?" I ask as I settle into the passenger side of her ride.

"No, but I think Emory got a phone call from her."

"Christ, that's something new. When?"

"This morning. He took the phone into the other room. The FBI picked it all up."

"Where is he now?"

"He's gone. He packed a bag and drove off. Said he was going to the airport. All I could get was the caller was asking for her to pay lots of money. More than ten million."

I have no idea what to make of that—the old boy may be heading for the South of France or Brazil—so I call Pax and fill him in. He can electronically track a snowflake through a snowstorm and I put him on it. He adds, "Mort said someone else had already bailed you when he called?"

"A beautiful brunette. And I know you're not surprised."

"Shocked, actually. I'll call when I have something on the Castiano properties and Coogan."

We find the Hampton Inn. I'm carrying a new pair of black Dockers that would pass for three-hundred-buck slacks, a pair of black Wranglers, two new pullovers that are dark enough to disappear if I have to do the creep, a three pack of black boxers, a six pack of socks, and a pair of black Reeboks with thick soles—shoes will nicely bury in the crotch of one of Castiano's boys but will move quiet.

The Hampton Inn has a shower over tub with room enough for both of us and a king size bed that turns out not to be quite big enough as we end up on the carpet. However, with this lady, a basketball court might not be big enough. She's a new woman and I'm glad I had a rematch or I would have misjudged her. I think my comment about removing Coogan's overbite stimulated her desire which in turn tuned up her performance.

I wish I'd gotten a better night's sleep in the hoosegow.

I'm happy to say my phone doesn't echo Ring of Fire across the room until I'm lying in a heap trying to catch my breath.

"Yeah," I answer, knowing it's Pax.

"We've emailed you a list of every Castiano related business and property we can find, and it's extensive. Your boy Coogan will be landing in Nashville in a couple of hours. He's booked on a return flight day after tomorrow."

"Have I told you lately that I love you," I say with a coo that gets a sour look from Tyler.

"Have I told you lately to go fuck yourself, and that has nothing to do with love," Pax replies.

"How about the van?"

"When do you want it there?"

"Tomorrow, noon. And bring me fifteen large in cash. I need some walking around dough and need to pay my brunette buddy back for bailing me."

"I'll have Sol drive it over. He's got family in Vacaville and wants to show off the Vette to his cousin." That makes Pax laugh.

"Tell the little chicken shit I'll make a capon out of him if he puts a scratch on it."

"You want to tell him?"

"No, he gets it. It's rumored the boys in Vegas have their claws deep in Coogan. Can you find out who and how much?"

"Will do. Is that why he borrowed from this Castiano?"

"Makes sense. It seems Tammy was smart enough not to loan it to him."

"I'll get back to you. You're having all the fun on this one."

"I'll yell if I need help."

He rings off.

Tyler is dressed, has touched up her makeup, and is doing the hair pat in front of the bathroom mirror, so I wander over and lean on the doorjamb. "You can pat for an hour and you can't get better than perfect."

"Well, well, aren't you the suave one."

"You look great, the only thing that looks better on you is nothing."

She leans over and gives me a smack on the lips, and goes back to patting.

"Why would Coogan go to Nashville?" I ask.

She shrugs. "We do lots of biz in Nashville. Tammy's bank and her accountant are in Nashville."

"Would Coogan forge a check on Tammy's account?"

She's silent for a moment, then turns to me. "I guess it depends upon how desperate he is. Nothing would surprise me. And if he's trying to get the money for Tammy's release, she'd want him to."

My phone goes off with Ring of Fire. "That didn't take long," I answer.

"Rocco's out in Henderson."

"What?"

"That's who had the markers from Coogan...and he couldn't pick worse guys to stiff. They're old school and have rumored to put a few in the sand. Emails on the server at Rocco's confirm Coogan paid up, after borrowing the dough from Castiano, who in turn borrowed from the Albanians, who are rumored to control Rocco's. Coogan probably jumped from the frying pan into the fire. It's a weird circle, but it's also well known the Albanians are trying to get a foothold into some Indian gaming in

California and will do anything to influence the politicians there. They bought a road building company in Arizona and Castiano is huge in road building in California. Who knows what they're thinking."

"Interesting. A true cluster fuck. All I got to worry about is getting Tammy back. But, thanks."

Tyler is out of the bathroom. "I've got to go back to the house. I'm supposed to stay close to the phone in case the guys who've got Tammy call again. Did you see the L.A. Times?"

"Nope."

"Front page on Tammy's abduction. Below the fold, but front page."

"So, no one's on the phone at the house?"

"The FBI has some stuff set up. When I told them I had to go they got call referral to me and said they'd be monitoring. But I got to get back."

"No Grill on the Alley supper?"

"Nope, I'm usually a dinner and drinks kind of girl, but you already came through with the goodies, so if you don't mind...."

"Hell, saves me a couple of hun. I'll owe you dinner, drinks, and a rematch."

"You're on, big boy. Let's go."

"And I was hoping you'd ride over to beautiful downtown Barstow with me."

"I can get you as far as the car impound in Malibu."

"I'll have your dough for you when I get back. Speaking of the FBI, I've got to give them a call."

She drives so I'm able to call Agent Quintana. She answers so it must be a cell.

"Quintana."

I'm surprised it's a female voice. I guess I should have known as it would have been Robert otherwise.

"Agent, Mike Reardon, you asked me to call."

"I'd like to chat a while, Reardon. Where are you?"

"Heading into the Santa Monica Mountains, on my way to Malibu."

"How about dropping by the Houston house?"

"I can be there in an hour or so. I've got to spring my wheels from the impound."

"How about coming here first. Is Tyler Thompson with you?"

"She's giving me a ride."

"Come here first, got it."

"Is there a please in there somewhere?"

"Yeah, please. But there won't be the next time I ask. There's also an APB out there for you if you don't show. Does that please you?"

"Yeah, I got it. It'll be my pleasure."

"Time marches on with this abduction. I'd like to find her alive."

Target Shy & Sexy

Chapter Twelve

Agent Quintana is a big lady who looks as if she can take care of herself. In fact she could play a pulling guard on the Chargers or Rams. I'd be surprised if she doesn't bench press more than I do. And she's no nonsense.

"You want coffee?" she asks when we pass the muster of an agent at the door.

"Sure," I say, as I'm hungry and the coffee will quell the appetite.

"Tea for me," Tyler says, then offers, "I'll make it. I know my way around."

We sit at a kitchen table made of the same granite as the countertops.

"So, Reardon, fill me in on how you fit into this scenario."

"No big mystery, agent. Tammy hired me over the phone…I used to work for her—"

"And she canned you, as I understand."

"Yes, but apparently she wised up and wanted my help when someone took a pot shot at her."

"We think the shot…both shots…were a scam to get her here to her beach house so they could snatch her."

"Makes sense. Particularly after they missed the second shot as well. Any decent rifleman could have taken her out if the shot came from where I think it did."

"Except for shooting through the glass."

"That's a factor. But I'll bet it was a fifty cal, and the glass wouldn't have been much, if anything, in the way of deflection."

"I see you had some sniper training in the Corps?"

"I did." Then I'm wondering, so I ask, "You wear the green?"

"I did, a dozen years. I served some of the same time you did."

"So you know I wouldn't have missed."

"You're not a suspect. You're also not part of this investigation. So stay away. Leave the Castianos alone, and take a ride back to Vegas. I'll call you if you're needed…not that I can imagine why. That's it. And don't distract Ms. Thompson anymore. She's needed here."

I rise. "Nice meeting you, agent."

"So, back to Vegas?"

"I've got business in California."

"Nowhere near my business if you're smart. I'd hate to bust a fellow Marine for obstructing justice."

I salute her but don't get one in return. I round the table and give Tyler a peck on the cheek.

"You'll call?" she asks.

I wave over my shoulder as I head for the door. "I'll call."

"After this is over," Quintana snaps.

"Semper fi," I say, and give her a wave over my shoulder. Elbow past the fibbie at the door, and I'm gone.

I no more than fire the Vette up when my phone rattles with an unknown caller ring.

"Reardon," I answer.

"Castiano here," the gruff voice replies.

"To what do I owe the dubious pleasure?"

"I understand you get things done?" he asks.

"Legal things…" then I qualify, "Or at least things I consider right."

"The assholes snatched my old lady."

"Margo?"

"Yes, Margo. I ain't no raghead. I only got one."

"And?"

"And I need your help. Are you still in California?"

"I'm a half mile from your place."

"Come on over. As they say on TV, let's make a deal."

"On my way. I gotta drive into Malibu first, so I'll be a while."

Tyler takes me to get my Vette and gives me a wet kiss when she drops me off.

The pencil-neck gateman waves me right on through. Tony eyes me dubiously as I park the Vette. Without so much as a good afternoon he shows me inside, this time to a library with ten-foot shelving and one of those rolling ladders, all surrounding a full-size snooker table with red felt to match red carpet but the carpet is patterned with fleur de lis in gold.

Tony shows me into the room, then leaves. Sammy has a tumbler of something in hand, and is leaning on the table. My new buddy Sergio is at the far end of the table, a pool cue in hand, looking like he'd like to use it on my noggin.

In a leather chair, with his knee in a cast, propped up on a bolster, is the guy whose knee I stomped, and he's not exactly giving me a welcome look.

"You met Sergio and Franco," Sammy says, and gives me a wink.

"Not officially," I say, and give both the boys a nod.

"Give us the room," Sammy says to his boys, and it's not a request. The one he called Franco stands with the help of Sergio and a crutch, and gimps out of the room with Sergio close behind.

"What can I do for you, Sammy?" I ask.

"You can do something for both of us."

"How's that?"

"The same guys who snatched your client snatched my old lady, so you can help us get them both back."

"You want me to work with frick and frack, and frack on crutches. No thanks."

"A quarter mil, you bring my old lady back. There's five of them. Fifty grand apiece for each one of them you put toes up. And there's a half dozen more over in Vegas, same price on their heads."

"These are the Albanian boys?"

"How'd you know that?"

"I've got my sources. How much do you owe them?"

He stares at me a moment, then mumbles. "Ten mil, plus the vig. They make it almost fifteen."

"And you loaned Coogan a mil when you owed the Albanian boys ten plus and you want me to believe you'll pay me a half mil, up to eight hundred or more, if I do your dirty work for you."

"It ain't just my dirty work. It's yours too."

"Why's Coogan in Nashville?"

"He's trying to cash a check drawn on Tammy's account. But it ain't gonna happen."

"Why not?"

"She's got plenty in the account, but he forged her sig and they ain't gonna cash no check without direct verbal authorization, probably at least a Skype face to face thing, from her. Coogan has a rep back there, and it ain't a lily white one."

"So, where are Tammy and Margo?"

"I got a good idea where, but we gotta shake first."

"She's in the country?" I ask.

"They are in the country, in fact if I'm right, in the state and not all that far. You gotta get my old lady...I don't give a rat's ass if you get Houston or not. That's your gig."

"Easy to say, but remember she's probably the only source of the mil plus Coogan owes you and you owe the Albanians."

"True, so save her sweet ass too."

I don't have anything to lose, so I walk around the table and extend my hand.

"We got no time to lose," Sammy says.

"I've got to go to Barstow in the morning. I'll be back late afternoon, and ready to rock and roll."

"Bullshit," he snaps. "We got no time to lose."

"I'm picking up some gear I'll need. Better to go prepared. Speaking of prepared, where do you think they are so I can get some recon started?"

"You know Paso Robles?"

"Sure, cow town turned yuppie wine town."

"I deeded them over the equity in a winery I owned up there, worth at least five mil for a chunk of what I owed them before…it started out at fifteen mil, I paid it down but it's back there again…and I have reason to believe that's where they got the ladies stashed. I still got some friends…old employees…up there. The scumbag Albanians gave me another seventy-two hours before they start sending Margo and Tammy back in chunks."

"Give me an address on the place and I'll get my people to work."

"I'll do better than that, I'll give you a set of plans. I built the place a dozen years ago."

"And the address, and the names and numbers of your 'friends' at the winery. When are you supposed to hear from Coogan to see if he's got some dough for you?"

"I'm surprised I haven't heard by now."

"I'm going to move up my meeting in Barstow." I glance at my watch and see it's almost five PM. "I'll be back here by two AM. Have the plans here and we'll go over them in the morning…early."

"Sergio and Franco will back you up."

"No deal, Sammy. My people will back me up."

"How many you got?"

"Two, besides myself, if I can get ahold of one of them. If not, then there'll only be two of us."

"These are bad motherfuckers," Sammy says, shaking his head.

"They may be bad, but my buddy's bad at a thousand yards. You gotta give me your word that Sergio and Franco will stay out of my play."

He looks dubious, but shrugs and nods his head. "I got seventy-two hours, I'll give you forty-eight."

"Get me the address."

"I got a plane at the Oxnard airport. Unless you gotta drive for some reason, how about my guy flies you to Barstow?"

"That'll work. You store my Vette and someone drives me to Oxnard. I'll drive myself back from Barstow in my rig."

"What's so important about this so-called rig?"

I laugh. "It's well rigged, that's what."

"Tony will drive you to the plane."

"Get me that address, and the names of anyone at the winery who might help."

Target Shy & Sexy

Chapter Thirteen

I call Pax on the way to the Oxnard airport and get things started, making sure he loads my Harley Iron in the van. All those lanes and two tracks in the vineyards and orchards, the bike might just come in handy. I also call my buddy Skip, who I call the Viking. Skip was with us in Desert Storm and went through some very bad stuff. He stays a little close to the bottle and has been known to test the water of hard drugs, but he's one of us and if I ask him to stay straight he will. And hand to hand I'll put him up against any four normal guys, bad or not. He also knows every weapon in our arsenal.

Sammy, my new employer, travels in style.

A turbo King Air is about as nice as it gets and I feel a little guilty riding in the back, alone, like some potentate so I right-seat it beside the pilot. He's a stoic cat who pays little attention to his passenger but lots of attention to his job, so I don't bother him with small talk.

Besides, it gives me time to think.

I got Sol on the way with my van after Pax loaded it up with select items from my ministorage, and put Pax onto the Castiano winery which is out Highway 46 only a few miles east of Paso Robles. Sol will bring the van directly onto the tarmac of the fixed base operator at Barstow so the pilot will be able to taxi right up next to the van, and I've talked Sammy into giving my little buddy a ride back to Vegas in the King Air. Sol will be pissed not to get the Vette to drive, but stoked about getting a ride in a classy airplane. And I put Pax onto a couple of Abanian names Sammy's provided me with.

Armand Ahmeti and Edvin Gashi are reported, by Sammy, to be number one and two in the Albanian Vegas hierarchy. And they have two dozen or more soldiers, a half-dozen of whom Pax has provided me with dossiers full of pictures and background info.

It's interesting how loyalties change. I was at odds with the Castiano family, and am now in bed with them, so to speak. A classic case of the enemy of my enemy is my friend. It'll be interesting to see if things have now leveled out and we know who the enemy actually is.

Not that Sammy is a friend, but he is a potential payday, and he is the enemy of my enemy, and that's close enough for the job at hand.

When I get back to the Castiano compound after the long drive and listening to a dozen country albums, some Katie Perry, and the total repertoire of the queen of the blues' Mamie Smith, who has the distinction of being the first African-American to record a vocal blues song, it's very late. The rusty old gal has a mystical quality about her voice and helped keep me awake. Someone did a great job of cleaning up recordings from 1920.

It's one thirty AM when I pull in the driveway and I'm pleased to see that Tony is waiting up for me. He offers to cook me something but I grabbed a burger on the way, so I pass. Not only did the plane make me feel like a potentate, but the guest room I'm ushered into is equally regal. Tony informs me he's already set the bedside alarm for five thirty AM as I'm to meet with Sammy for breakfast and to go over the plans at six.

Five thirty comes pretty damned early, but I shower and shave—I hate to go into an op unshaven as the thought of some mortician shaving me gives me the willies—and dress in jungle camo as I suspect I'll be doing some recon from out in the vineyards. Skip is flying into Paso in the late afternoon and Pax will charter over if I can't get Sammy to send a plane for him, should I decide I'll need him. And I'm sure I will.

Sammy is a detail guy, and we go over the plans...hide, hair, bones and all. He also fills me in on his former ranch manager who stayed on to work for the Albanians and still lives in a foreman's house on the easterly of the two sections of Castiano Winery. Only four hundred or so acres are developed to Zinfandel, Cabernet Sauvignon and Merlot, while one-sixty is planted with apples. By the Google Earth pics, I've looked at the apples and the vineyards are mature. Sammy had plans to get into hard cider as well as wine. The balance of the property is covered with scattered oak and grazing land.

Sammy talked about the place with reverence and it's clear it tore a chunk out of his fat heart when he had to give it up.

I'm enjoying the ride up the coast through Malibu, inland past Oxnard, the coast again from Ventura to a few miles north of Santa Barbara, and then slightly inland at Gaviota Pass, past

93

the quaint town of Solvang, on to Santa Maria, the five cities touching the coast again, then inland again to San Luis Obispo, past Atascadero and finally roll into Paso Robles. The Pacific I've passed is quiet, slow heaves of ocean dotted with floating kelp and occasional seabirds floating while others skim the water close enough that if they dropped their feet they'd be wet. Far out there's a bank of clouds, and it portends a change in the weather. I was kind of wishing I were riding the Harley, but the possible change in weather is changing my thinking. I'm on Highway 101 all the way until, almost through Paso Robles, I turn east onto Highway 46 where Castiano Winery resides, one of the largest of two dozen wineries flanking both sides of the highway.

I'm a wine fan, nothing like a great Cab Sav or Malbec with a thick steak, but I'm no snob. Many ten-buck bottles I've enjoyed more than one some snob has paid a Franklin for. However, I'm looking forward to taking a tour of the Castiano operation. Some wineries have rodent problems and I plan to clean the rats out of this one if they get in my way.

I made a drive-by of the place, impressed with a stone gate and rose-bush-lined wide driveway leading to a tasting room of the same stone that formed the wide-arched entry gate. There's a stylish twenty-foot-wide sign announcing "Wine tasting and tours." A half-dozen cars and an RV are in the lot, I presume partaking of the goodies and being softened up so they'll overpay for some vino. A hundred yards beyond the tasting room is the winery itself. I drive a half-mile beyond the gate and spot a service road and what I know from Sammy is the vineyard manager's residence. It's a simple stucco with a composition roof, probably three bedrooms and one bath for Enrico Ramos and his wife and three kids. Bikes and trikes and a plastic kiddy pool litter the yard. My contact, hopefully, at Castiano.

I return on the far side of Highway 46 and pull off on a crown in the road where I dig my binocs out of the center console and can see over the vineyards, now flush with bright green spring growth.

The winery building is at least a half-acre in size, and stone too, at least on the side facing the road. It backs up to a bank rising about thirty feet, and is partly dug into the hill. I know from studying the plans that they've dug a cave into the hill—what's a winery without a cave—where they age wine in scorched French oak.

Next to the winery building is a crushing pad with a ramp where trucks can dump the harvest. The fruit travels via conveyors into a stemmer crusher and the juice moves on via stainless steel piping into thousand-gallon stainless fermentation tanks. Then maceration takes place and the mixture of juice and skins are heated to release color from the skins in the case of red wines. The pressing of the mixture releases pure red juice, which still needs to be filtered.

On the west side of the building are two three-sided six foot high bins of concrete block, each containing a few tons of material. Diatomaceous earth makes up one huge pile, used for filtering; bentonite clay another, used for fining or giving the solids in the wine something to cling to so they'll sink to the bottom of the fining barrels or tanks. Only after some additions does the wine go to oak barrels to be aged. On top of the rise three hundred yards to the west are a half-dozen cottages which must house farm labor. Not fancy, but clean and neat.

In the distance, with only a tile roof visible from the highway, is a residence and guest house surrounded by large California sycamore trees. I know the residence to be at least seven thousand square feet, two stories in its middle section with two one-story wings jutting out at forty-five degree angles, and a guest house on the far side of a large swimming pool and Jacuzzi. The guesthouse I know from the plans to be a two bedroom affair, two in-bath suites separated by great room, kitchen, and dining room.

I can understand why Sammy was remorseful.

After a cursory drive-by, a u-turn, another drive-by and stop with the binocs, I move on up the highway back toward Paso Robles. Wanting to kill a little time as the same van going back and forth might attract attention, I go to a drive-thru and get a fish sandwich and a cup of coffee, then return and again drive past the main entrance a half-mile to the drive leading to the Ramos residence. I pull the van off the road and raise the hood so it appears that I have car trouble, then hoof it the two hundred yards to the house.

Mrs. Ramos is a pleasant, rotund little woman with bright black eyes and a pair of kids peering out, one on each side of flaring hips wrapped in a stained apron. She has flour on her hands, and brushes them as she smiles at me.

"Is Mr. Ramos in?" I ask.

"Señor Ramos...garage," she says, and points to the side of the house. It's obvious to me her English is limited. I smile and nod and walk the way she's pointed. A white pickup, new with Castiano Winery and a bunch of purple grapes emblazoned on the door, is parked in the house driveway in front of a single-car garage door, but beyond is a thirty by sixty foot shop building and two guys are working on a tractor-pulled spray rig with high booms that would cover at least three rows on either side of the rig. So I head that way.

"Mr. Ramos," I call out as I approach, as either of them could be.

A solid-looking Hispanic, six inches shorter than me but equally as wide, and with callused and scarred hands that look like they started with a shovel handle when he was about nine, steps forward and offers one of those stubby hands.

He's a gentle shaker but I get the impression he could crush rocks if he had the urge.

"Sí," he says.

"You got a moment? I need to talk."

He nods and we walk thirty feet to the shade of a fruitless mulberry, leaving the other guy to his work.

"I'm Dick Strong, a friend of Mr. Castiano," I say, by way of introduction.

"Señor Sammy, he called me," he says. "But he said Mike somebody was coming?"

I ignore that, and continue. "He's worried about Mrs. Castiano. He thinks she may be here, held against her will. Have you seen her...and another young blonde woman?"

"I no see, but I think maybe...."

"Maybe?"

"Maybe she here."

"She, or two ladies?"

He shrugs.

"So," I ask, "why do you think she might be here?"

"Cars come and go late at night. When no workers. Food is taken to the aging cave and no one allowed to the deep storage."

"That's in the back of the aging cave?"

"Sí."

"Guards?"

"Two, always at the back of the cave. One outside. He leaves at night after the guests depart."

"There's a room at the back of the cave?"

"A big room. Doors big enough to drive into and a man size door. Something strange goes on."

"Okay, Enrico...May I call you Enrico?"

"Sí." He's silent for a moment, then adds, "Señor Sammy, he very good to us. New owners not so much. But I work them. I need job."

"I won't be back, Enrico. My van is out on the road. Tell anyone who asks that I had car trouble and asked for help. Otherwise, you've never seen me."

He nods and looks very worried, so I add, "Stay clear of the winery tonight, in fact it would be a good night to visit relatives somewhere else."

He nods again. Then he smiles and suggests. "Two ways into cave. The new owners have us dig another way in and out. No guard there."

"Where?"

"Pump house on top of hill. Ladder from inside goes down to room in back. We use old three-foot culvert for walls. Don't tell I told, por favor."

"Thanks, amigo."

"Señora Castiano a good woman. She kind to mi esposa. Be careful."

"Go to town tonight."

"Sí."

I shake again, and head back to the van. It was well worth the stop.

Now for a little closer recon, and a look at this new cave access, if I can get to it without being seen.

Chapter Fourteen

My buddy Skip is coming in on a 5:10 PM flight, so I don't have a lot of time. I find a two track off a side road which leads to within a hundred yards of the back property line of the Castiano property, and work my way there, parking in a small copse of scrub oaks. I carry a number of magnetic signs hidden in the side panels of the van, but none of them point to a good reason the van might be parked in a fairly open field, so I choose a Paladin Pest Control pair and affix them to the sides of the van. Maybe they'll think I'm exterminating ground squirrels. I figured a 'have gun will travel' approach a good one for a pest control guy.

I've noticed that most the farm workers are in jeans and blue denim work shirts, and I have jeans and don them, over an ankle holster with a small Ruger .380 therein. I don't want to be seen carrying a long arm, but also have no interest in being defense-naked. My shirt, however, doesn't look like farm worker, but is rather a black pullover. My boots look military, because they are...but hell, lots of guys wear camo boots these days.

It's a full half-mile through the vineyards and a corner of the apples to the pump house I'm particularly interested in. Another of the spray rigs, like the one Enrico was overhauling, is running through the vineyards, but I'm sure the driver will have little if any interest in me, so I charge forward down a lane with Zinfandel on one side and Cab Sav on the other, until I reach the apple orchard then duck into it and make my way through trees only a couple of feet taller than my six two. I've given the main house and its guesthouse a wide berth.

The apples are not normal tree shape but have been trimmed to be flat on either side, I presume for mechanical harvest. I have to duck to move from row to row, but am soon in sight of the green metal roof of the small ten by ten metal building that Enrico has said houses not only pumping and electrical equipment but an access to the cave below. I boldly cross the twenty feet from orchard to building.

The damn door has a hardened padlock, and this damn fool left his lock pick set in the van. Seldom are outbuildings on farms locked, so although it's a bad thing I can't get in, it may be a good thing as it means there's something to hide.

Okay, plan two.

There's a fresh new set of vehicles in the parking lot of the tasting room, a half-dozen cars and two pickups pulling travel trailers.

So I boldly charge forward.

I have to sidle through a protective row of rose bushes, and am surprised when a no-neck is parked in a canvas backed chair just inside a row of grape vines, and he challenges me as soon as I step out of the roses.

"Hey, pardner, what the hell are you doing?" He unlimbers from the chair. His loose shirt is un-tucked, but it's obvious he's carrying by the lump on his right hip.

I do my best sheepish tourist imitation, and stammer. "I was on a tour and had to take a leak."

"Nobody wanders away from the tour. Get your ass back there."

"Yes, sir," I say. "Sorry."

"Get back there."

So I jog the hundred yards to the tasting room, past the concrete wall bins of material and the main winery building. Just as I reach the parking lot, a group of eight are leaving with a sweet little strawberry blonde college-age girl leading a tour, so I give them all a smile and join right in taking up a position at the back of the pack. I glance back up to the hill where the no-neck has returned to his chair, and give him a wave and a smile. I get a glare in return and no wave...rude bastard.

It's a nice group of folks I'm tagging along with, and the cutest little college-age button-nose leading the pack, and explaining the wine-making process. She's giving me more than one come-hither glance, but as she looks to be about seventeen and as I'm a little preoccupied, I ignore her. As she fills her tight red blouse nicely and wears those skin-tight, reveal every nook and cranny, skinny jeans that compliment a perfectly protruding gluteus maximus, I'm showing some real will power. We get past the stemmer and leaf remover, the crusher, the various tanks, and finally to where the oak barrels are filled. Each of us gets a taste from glass gizmo that's dipped into a barrel and watch as a special forklift moves barrels back onto racks in the cave. For the first time I crowd to the head of the group, which stops only about twenty feet into the cave.

At the end, about sixty feet, I see another no-neck, also in a canvas seat director's chair. He's carefully eying our group, but seems relaxed. He's next to the double truck-wide doors Enrico described, and on his far side is a people pass-through door. The double doors have a large hasp, but no lock thereon, and the pass through door has only a bedroom type lock, I presume, as I can see the tiny hole for the tool to turn and unlock an accidentally locked door. Lousy security.

When the tour is over we retire to the tasting room, but I fade to the back of the group and don't follow. Instead I disappear around the side of the building, on the far side away from the view of the outside guard. Slipping into the rose bushes, I'm out the other side and into a vineyard.

But this time I'm going to make a close pass by the big house and guesthouse.

At least that's my plan, until I hear the dogs barking.

Another fine plan goes awry.

So I stay over two hundred yards from the house and hustle back to the van.

It takes me over a half hour to get through the vineyards and back to where I'm sure I've left the van.

I'm more than just a little surprised to wander out of the vineyard to see a sheriff's patrol car parked next to my van, and a deputy with a flashlight peering into one of the two rear door windows.

"Can I help you," I yell from a hundred feet away.

He's careful, and turns with a hand on the semi-auto on his hip.

"What's going on here?" he asks, his tone demanding.

"Sightseeing, checking out the vineyards."

"You're on private property."

I get close and extend my hand, which he doesn't accept, showing him a stupid smile and reading his name tag. "Sorry, Officer Brownley, I didn't see any signs."

"You in the pest control business?"

"Sure enough. I'm thinking of moving over this way. I was looking for thrips or spider mites to see if I could stir up some business."

He's quiet for a moment, then, as my hand is still extended, finally takes it and shakes. "Believe it or not folks steal lots of grapes right off the vine."

"Probably not until they ripen up some," I say, with a laugh.

"No, probably not. You got a name?"

I'm thinking about which driver's license I have in my wallet, then remember. "Dick Strong, from Nevada. Looking to move to Paso Robles."

"Got a driver's license?" he asks.

I flip it out and am happy to see I've remembered which one I'm carrying. He eyeballs it quickly and doesn't even ask me to remove it. Then he adds, "Welcome to Paso. Good luck with stirring up some business. Should be lots of work around."

"Thanks," I say, and head for the driver's seat.

"Follow the same tracks out. Folks don't want new ruts cut into their ground."

"You bet. Thanks officer."

I'm not sure he's convinced that my intentions were honorable, but at least I'm on my way to pick up Skip, and not on my way to the hoosegow. I hate to attract the attention of the law, particularly in sight of someplace where I'm about to break the law, but que sera.

It's about time to pick up Skip, and I hope he's straight and sober.

Target Shy & Sexy

Chapter Fifteen

The Paso Robles Municipal Airport is not hard to find if you take Airport Road as a hint. It's east of Paso as is Castiano Winery, and just a couple of miles north of Highway 46.

I'm waiting at the curb as I know Skip, and Skip doesn't travel with checked baggage unless he's going to be gone for several months. And it's not like the boy is hard to spot in a crowd, at six-foot-five and somewhere between two-sixty and two-eighty he literally stands above the crowd. Skip's blonde, and if you looked up Viking in the dictionary you're likely to see his picture. He is bearded, but it's nicely trimmed and his hair's cut, so I hope and pray he's on a good streak—off the booze and not looking for help in a one-gram vial. Even more than Pax and me, he came out of desert storm with lots of nightmares, the worst of which was chasing a Haji into a mud hut and chucking a grenade into a back room rather than going in balls out and taking a few rounds from an AK47. The bad news was the bad guy got away out a back door, the far worse news was a one year old and three year old who were sleeping in the room didn't get away. Skip's still haunted. Anyone would be.

But he's a great guy, and one of us, and as such we'd do about anything for each other.

He opens the slider on the side of the van, throws in his carry-on size duffle, jumps into the passenger seat, then extends a ham size hand which I take reluctantly as I know he carries rock crushers on the end of each Popeye forearm.

"What's the gig?" he asks without bothering with howdy or how the hell are you.

"Some very bad boys have absconded with a lady I used to work for and another lady from down Malibu way."

He gives me a suspicious glance. "Are we recovering a lost love or is this real work?"

"Sammy Castiano, one of our employers, owes some boys from Vegas, some Albanian boys who bury those who don't pay up. They snatched Sammy's wife...his seventy year old wife...and say they'll send her back in small packages in..." I glance at my watch, "in sixty hours or so if he doesn't come through with fifteen mil." I pull away from the curb and head back to the highway.

"And he's paying us to get her back?"

"That's the rumor. And do you remember me telling you I'd worked for Tammy Houston, the country singer?"

"Yeah, and I remember that didn't work out too well for you."

"Yeah, it didn't. However she called me and wanted me to come back to work as someone was taking pot shots at her. When I showed up, she'd been snatched by these same Albanian boys. It seems the pot shots were to get her out of her guarded condo and out to the boondocks in Malibu."

"How does all this tie together?"

"It's a little weird. Castiano loaned Tammy's manager some dough and he didn't pay it back. The Albanians probably figured that Tammy, who Forbes Magazine said was knocking down five mil a month, could pay and might even loan Castiano the money to pay back the major dough he owed. The best we can figure, Castiano got way upside down on some road-building project.... He owns an engineering contracting company. Anyway, they snatched his old lady and Tammy and I guess have told the manager, a creep named Coogan, to cough up the dough. Tammy has it, but the manager can't get his hands on it. Anyway, let's spring the ladies then let them sort it all out without the women travelling home in small packages."

"How bad are these Albanians?"

"Zero inhibitions. Tons of aggression. Bad, bad, bad boys, or so Pax reports."

"So, if they go down, so be it."

"So be it."

We drive a while before I ask. "So, you doin' okay? You off the sauce and the nose candy?"

"Yeah." He says, and that's enough for me.

I head back into town so I can find a quiet spot to go over the details with Skip. So far it doesn't look to be too tough, so I don't bother to call Pax for additional backup. Pax's strong suit is the sniper rifle, and the layout is such the only really long range shots would have to be across Highway 46, which is not a particular problem, particularly at night, but the California Highway Patrol and the county sheriff's deputies patrol the highway. No reason to irritate folks unless absolutely necessary, and a .308 cutting the air overhead could be a minor irritation.

After I brief Skip we make another drive by the winery and give him a firsthand view of the layout. Then we have to kill some time as I don't plan to go into a well-guarded facility in daylight. Let's give these boys a chance to suck on a bottle and get heavy eyes.

Skip suggests a few beers to kill some time and I don't know if he's kidding or not…he knows I never drink when going into an op. He laughs it off, and I'm glad he does.

Since he hasn't seen the place, we re-sign the van with Pacific Plumbing signs and I hide out in the back—where there's a cot, sink, and small 12-volt refrigerator—and take a nap while he does a tour with the promise he won't partake more than a sip at the tasting bar. It's a little crowded in back of the van with the Harley taking up more than its share, but I manage.

Skip catches the last tour of the day—making note of the same things I saw—then we head back into town, and, with nothing else to do, catch a movie at the local multiplex. We're out at nine and then go to supper at a local buffet. He eats like a horse, as usual, and I snack as my stomach is always full of worms before an op, and tonight is no different.

Finally, at midnight, we strip the signs off the van, again becoming vanilla plain, and suit up in Kevlar vests, black pants, and long sleeve black pullovers. Skip wears night vision goggles on a Kevlar helmet, just in case we need that advantage. I slip on a black knit cap. We go light with the arms, each of us with a 40 mm Glock and a backup ankle pistol—mine a lightweight 5 shot Ruger .38 and Skip with a small Ruger .380 semi-automatic—a belt loop with a can of mace, and a sap. We don't go with the full battle rattle belt as I hope silence is the answer to this op, but I do clip a pair of flash grenades onto my web belt. We both have Motorola radios with ear buds, set on channel 07 for luck. Skip is entrusted with a small pair of bolt cutters, not enough to handle a hardened lock but enough to snip the chain on normal cuffs. We also each have several cable ties, which will serve as restraints should we need them.

I work my way back to the rear of the property only this time don't leave the van in the copse of oak trees, but rather kill the lights and drive right down between the vineyards to the edge of the apple orchard. I get the van reversed and headed out in case we have to make a quick getaway. If we're able to spring the ladies—if they're actually there—then I can't imagine hustling them through a half mile of vineyards back to the van. No telling what kind of condition they're in. As it is we're only a couple of hundred yards from the pump building that is supposed to house the vertical culvert that's a secret access to the room at the back of the aging cave.

We work our way through the apples and this time I have my lock pick kit at hand. It's a decent hardened lock—too much for the bolt cutters—and takes me almost fifteen minutes to pick.

I'm wondering if the guard is still posted outside overlooking the parking lot and tasting area, but there's no real reason to move to the slope and take a look. Why risk being seen?

Then I find it's not necessary to take a look, as just as I get the lock to spring, Skip taps me on the shoulder and whispers. "Guard, looks like he's on patrol."

I spot him and he's walking on top the slope, a path that will take him only a few feet from where we crouch behind the pump building. Skip eyes him via the night goggles and reports, "Combat shotgun, side arm." The question is, will he check the door.

If it were an access to where I had the goods hidden, I would check the door.

We'll see.

Just as he gets within twenty feet of us, the sky opens up and the storm that the clouds promised arrives. I smile as he spins on a heel and begins to jog back the way he came, the rain beating down on him and already forming puddles. It's a deluge.

The weather gods are with us.

We slip into the building and in a corner is a three-foot diameter vertical culvert just as Enrico described, and a ladder inside disappears into the darkness. With the ladder taking up six inches, it's a tight fit for Skip, so I suggest he hang back and make sure the guard doesn't stumble in and catch us in the hole. We'd be a hard target to miss stuffed into a three-foot pipe.

I descend over twenty feet before I hit bottom, and my pen light shows a door, not fancy, just cut out of the side of the culvert with hinges welded on so it will swing aside. There is a quarter-inch gap around the door and I realize there's just a smidgen of light coming from whatever is beyond.

Then I hear voices. "Change the fucking channel, Vito. I'm tired of this shit."

And then a female voice, slightly slurred, "Yeah, asshole, change the fucking channel."

The voice sounds like Margo Castiano, her sweet gentle own self.

A second male voice, I presume Vito, snarls, "Shut the fuck up you dried up old bitch. I hope your old man don't pay up so I can cut your sloppy tits off and feed them to the hogs."

"Eat shit, asshole," Margo replies, her voice again slurred. She may have floppy tits, but she's got big balls.

So, there's more than one of them.

But how many? And I was hoping I'd catch them asleep. The weather gods were with us, but the sleep gods seem to be working against us.

Chapter Sixteen

Fools rush in where angels fear to tread.

I don't plan to stay in this hole—did I mention I'm a little claustrophobic?—for any longer than I absolutely have to, so there's no waiting for the TV watchers to nod off. As I don't know where the women might be, I don't want lead flying around the room—Sammy might be a little upset if I brought Margo back full of holes. I palm the mace can and flip the little protective cover off. Then I whisper into the radio. "I'm going balls out."

"10-4," comes back.

I free one of the flash grenades from my web belt, give the door a shove, but only four inches, and it squeaks like a ruptured duck, pull the pin and count three as I hear a voice, "What the hell?" and roll the grenade into the room. I turn away and cover my ears and feel the shock of the explosion as I fill my right hand with the Glock and ready the mace in my left. I try and shove

111

the door open enough to pass through, but it sticks and I have to put my back to the wall and kick the hell out of it, and only then charge through.

Two guys had been playing cards, drinking cans of beer, and watching the tube. Both are stumbling around, one on his knees, and filling their hands with semi-autos from their belts.

I charge ten feet into the room and go to work with the mace—luckily they're still stunned from the grenade—hitting the standing guy, who's about Skip's size, full in the face and he roars and covers his eyes with both hands, one still holding his semi-auto pistol. He's gasping like a guppy in stagnant water.

The other guy is on his knees, taking deep racking breaths like an asthmatic and shaking his head back and forth trying to focus his vision and stop the reverberation of his eardrums. The flash grenade has done its work. I gas him full in the face, step up and swing a boot into the side of his head and the pistol flies across the room, skittering on the concrete floor. He goes down to his side, crying like a scalded cat and rubbing at his eyes.

The first guy can't see or breathe, but he's panning the semi-auto around the room like he might have a target. I use my own Glock as a club and bring the butt of the grip down on his wrist. His pistol goes to the floor and I kick it away to join the other one.

It's time to make this end so I holster my Glock, palm my sap, and crack him on the side of the head. He's an animal, and only goes to his knees, so I crack him even harder and this time he hits the floor like a sack of rocks, unmoving.

They're both out cold, but I want a little insurance so I do their wrists behind their backs with the cable ties and drag one close enough to the other that I can cable tie them together. They're still gasping and coughing, and tears pour from their eyes.

Only then do I survey the room. It's lit only by a desk lamp on a card table, now covered with loose playing cards, and the TV that's showing a rerun of some old movie.

There are two cyclone fence cages against the back wall—they remind me of prefab dog kennels. In one Margo Castiano is sitting on her butt on the cold concrete, trying to rub the flash out of her eyes. The other one is standing with door open, and vacant.

Where the hell is Tammy Houston?

I hustle to Margo's door, also cyclone fence, and find it locked and chained but this time it's a simple Master lock. I could probably pic it about as quickly, but instead hustle back to the culvert access and radio up to Skip to throw down the bolt cutters.

And get no answer.

So I call out just in case the radio has failed. "Skip! Where the hell are you?"

Nothing.

Where the fuck is Skip?

So I hustle back and pick the lock. I help Margo to her feet then notice a half-empty quart bottle of hooch on the floor next to where she was sitting.

"Margo, we've got to go," I say.

"Go where?" she stammers, and I realize she's hoot owl drunk.

"Out of here. You like that cage?"

She giggles. Jesus, I'm dealing with a drunken woman, my partner is missing, and I've got a twenty-foot ladder to climb. Fuck.

"Margo. These guys were going to cut you into kabobs and send you back to your old man in little packages...after they feed your boobs to the pigs. I'd suggest you sober up so we can get the hell out of here."

"Les' go. I remember you. You wouldn't take a Jacuzzi with me."

"Move it." I shove her to the culvert door and inside. She has on flip-flops, which are not exactly ladder-climbing gear. "Kick off the go-aheads and start climbing."

113

"I can't climb that fuckin' ladder," she stammers.

"Well, I can, and I'm leaving your drunken ass here if you don't get with it. You wanna go back to your Jacuzzi, right?"

"Okay, okay…here I go."

If you've never tried to climb a ladder in a narrow space with your shoulder in an older lady's crotch, while she's missing every other rung and falling back on you, you just haven't lived. It takes us a full ten minutes, and I have no idea what I'm going to find at the top…but we get there and she flops on her butt on the cold concrete floor of the pump house, and giggles. I am busy panning my Glock wondering where the hell my partner is, and finding no one.

I go to the doorway and study the dark landscape outside. It's still raining, but not a deluge as before. Nothing. Skip has disappeared.

I drag Margo through the dark, working our way through the apples, ducking and dodging while she bitches and moans. My first business is to save the woman, so I haul ass out of there. As we hit the highway, I aim the van toward Paso and my first call is to Sammy.

"I got your lady."

"Thank God. She okay?"

"She's been nursing her woes with a bottle, but she seems fine. Come get her."

"We'll pick her up…where? The Paso airport?"

"I've got to go back to the winery. I'm missing a buddy and haven't found Tammy. I'm not taking Margo to the airport as they may look for us there. There's a Hampton Inn in town. I'll call you with a room number when I check her in."

"I don't want you to leave her."

"I got no choice, Sammy. I got other business. My buddy may be in bad trouble."

"She'd better be there."

"Just get your ass up here and get her."

I ring off and immediately call Pax, who I awaken.

"Where do I bail you out this time?" he answers without bothering with hello. He's obviously not so sleepy he can't read caller ID.

"Skip is missing. Get your ass over here. I've only got one flash left, so stock up but make it quick. This may be balls out so bring what you think we need." I don't want to go into detail over a cell phone, and don't have to as Pax will come ready for a small war.

"I'll charter and call you when I touch down."

I get Margo checked in using one of my phony driver's licenses, then call Sammy with the room number.

If these Albanian a-holes have hurt my buddy Skip, I plan to bring their whole world down on them.

Target Shy & Sexy

Chapter Seventeen

I think it's time to make a move on the main house, as it's the obvious place for him to be if they got the drop on him...but I remember barking dogs when I formerly got close. And dogs are difficult to deal with. I like dogs, and hate the thought of putting a couple down that are only doing their jobs. I'm sure that's where they'll have Tammy stowed as well, as they've lost one woman and don't want to lose another without getting paid what's owed.

Going straight to an all-night minimarket, I hope I find the solution to the mutts.

I buy two bottles of hydrogen peroxide, a half-dozen meat burritos, and some sandwich bags. I fill the bags about a third with peroxide and tie them tight, making a small balloon of liquid peroxide, then carefully place one in the center of each burrito. Now if I can get close enough to the hounds without being eaten, maybe I can coax them into partaking of a little doctored Mexican chow. Upchucking dogs are usually interested in little else while they're emptying their stomachs, then shortly the other end, on the lawn.

Torn between going straight to the Castiano main house or waiting for Skip, I decide to actually use my head and get some backup before I storm the castle ramparts. It's a long two and a half hour wait until I get a call on the cell, and the phone spits out Ring of Fire and I know it's Pax.

"Ten minutes out," he says.

"Good. Lax security at the Paso airport so I'll be on the tarmac at Central Coastal, the FBO. We gotta get there before light if there's any way. So haul ass into the van."

"10-4," he replies.

And he does, but he has to make two trips from plane to van as he's got three four foot long duffle bags as freight, and they're all three full. He brought enough stuff to storm nearby Fort Hunter Liggett Army Base.

We roar off to the winery.

"So, what's in your bags of tricks?"

"Hell, a little bit of everything. An RPG being the biggest. Two M4's with four clips each—.223's with Picatinny rail systems, Grip Pod vertical forward grip, both with M68 CCO sights. I also brought the .308 with night vision. Two battle-rattle belts. Kevlar vests. Grenades…shock and fragmentation. Combat shotgun, M15g with grenade launcher. Standard stuff."

"You da man," I say and we're silent as we roar east on Highway 46, and as Pax studies the layout of the house on the plans Sammy has provided.

He finally looks up, "Any idea at all where they might have Skip?"

"If they have him, and haven't planted him out in the orchard somewhere. And I still don't have the lady."

"They've got a wine cellar as big as a three-car garage. That would be my guess if you want to keep someone out of sight of the help, and I'll bet they have lots of help."

I glance at my watch. It's five AM and the sun is beginning to lighten the eastern sky in front of us.

We gotta move.

I've decided it's best to split up. Me on the Harley, Pax with the van.

I sling an M4 over my shoulder, strap on my vest and battle-rattle, load my sack of burritos into a saddle bag, and when we get to the west edge of the winery take a two track until I think we're about even with the main house. We both have radios with ear buds. Giving Pax instructions about how to get around to the back, and down the lane closer to the house, I fire up the Harley and take a ride into the vineyards—not on a road but between the rows of vines.

I get close then idle to within a hundred yards of the house and park the Harley Iron as deep under the vineyard wires and vines as I can get it. I'm walking into a sky beginning to show a line of orange at the horizon. We don't have much time if darkness is to be our friend.

The dogs begin to bark before I get fifty yards from the yard. As best I can tell, the front of the house is behind a six or seven-foot plastered wall, probably concrete block. The back, however, is a cyclone wire fence mostly covered with wisteria. When I'm only six feet from the fence, two very large, obviously angry, Dobermans are bouncing off the fence trying to get to my throat. I plop down, cross-legged, and work to look harmless and content as Buddha and commune with the doggie gods, waiting until they begin to tire of barking and are reduced to growling.

Only then do I move forward and drop a burrito over the fence.

At first they ignore it, having returned to a vicious cacophony of barks, which they keep up for at least five minutes. Again, they're reduced to growling, until one of them sniffs the burrito, then in two bites, it's gone. This time when I approach the fence, it's only growling, and I drop two more. Dobe One eats his second and Dobe Two his first. Again I approach and the growls are barely discernable. The final three burritos barely bounce on the turf before they're in doggie darkness, and barely out of sight before Dobe One begins to stagger a little, then retch, then projectile vomit.

I activate the radio and give Pax a heads up. "Dogs handled. You in place?"

"10-4."

Dobe Two almost immediately follows suit with the upchucking, and as I vault the fence, neither dog pays me any mind. Both are busily emptying their stomachs and I know they will be for some time. Hydrogen peroxide and doggie stomachs don't mix. They'll be no worse for the wear, but it'll be tomorrow or next week before they think of Mexican food again.

I have to skirt a large swimming pool to reach the house, but then I'm deep in some shrubbery, my eyes trying to make sense of the interior of the house in the darkness. Obviously there are no motion detectors scanning the lawn or the dogs would set them off.

The Albanians are not early risers.

I'm looking into a rec room and know from the plans that it has two sliding doors out onto the pool patio, and also has a bathroom with shower and a pass through door to the outside. I'd already decided that the bathroom is my portal to the inside. I'm sure the sliders are alarmed, but the bathroom door may not be as it's got both a deadbolt and a lock on the knob.

Pax has had plenty of time to get set up on the corner of the property—the house, pool and guest house are inside a two-acre fenced area—and it's the high side, almost ten feet above the opposite corner offering him the best field of fire. He has both an M4 and the .308 with both night vision scope and open sights when the scope's removed from the rails.

It only takes me five minutes to pick both locks, but it's Murphy's law, and all hell breaks loose when I open the door. I have the presence of mind to lock them behind me even with the blaring of sirens and bells in my ears. If they've killed Skip and Tammy, even they are awakened by the alarms. I sprint across the rec room to where there's a sixteen foot wet bar with eight or ten stools, and duck behind it.

It's only thirty seconds before I hear two guys running down a hallway, shouting at each other. One enters the rec room and heads straight for the bathroom. The alarm system obviously identifies the area of intrusion.

I can see between the crack of a small swinging door that opens into the wet bar and watch the guy as the room light comes on and he moves into the bath, a semi-auto in hand.

In seconds he yells back. "No one here. No break-in. Doors are locked. Must have been that fucking cat again."

"Check outside," one voice says, and I hear a sliding door roll open.

I can't help but smile. You gotta love cats that set off house alarms.

Then another voice comes from the hall. "What's going on?"

I take the opportunity to whisper into the radio, "Company coming."

And get a whispered, "10-4."

"It's okay, Mr. Gashi. Go on back to bed. We got this."

"Bullshit. What's up?"

"It's just that damned cat again. If your old lady—"

"Watch your mouth, Fitor."

"Yes, sir."

"Did Rostov get here yet? I want this big blonde asshole out of here. Anybody find his car yet?"

"No sir."

"And no sign of the Castiano woman?"

"No, sir. We figure Sammy and his boys got her and are long gone."

"And the big guy?"

"Hired help. He keeps saying he's just a burglar and was by himself, but that's bullshit as common thieves don't wear no five grand night vision. I figure they don't give a shit about him. Sammy got his old lady back. We'll head back down and twist blonde boy's tail some more when we make sure things are good here."

Gashi growls, "Yeah, Sammy's happy…until we waste them all."

"You ready for us to go to work on the singer bitch? She's scared shitless watching us work the big blonde guy over. We should get the plane over here and haul her to Nashville if that's where she's got dough."

"I'll think about that. I'm gonna call her manager first. I'd way rather have my dough than croak her ass. And hauling her around the country is dangerous."

"Okay."

"But first," the guy called Gashi says, "I'm gonna get me a couple more hours of zees."

"Yes, sir. We're on this. Bosco is checking the grounds, just to make sure."

I'm beginning the cramp up, kneeling behind the bar for fifteen minutes, watching the only guy left in the room as he walks to a far wall, picks up a tuner and clicks on CNN to take in the early morning news. He's got dirty blonde hair, and if his dark eyebrows are an indication, it's dyed. He either had a hell of a case of smallpox as a kid, or his acne ran amuck as his face is the surface of the moon.

Finally he walks to the still-open sliding door and yells out. "Bosco, what the hell are you doing?"

And he gets no answer. I imagine Bosco made the mistake of strolling past a bush where Pax was laying low, and now Bosco is laying even lower.

He yells again. The guy Gashi referred to as Fitor has holstered his weapon, so I don't worry about confronting him, so long as he doesn't yell out. He's a little under six feet, but V-shaped and was either born with the body of a running back or spent a lot of time pushing weights.

He moves back to the pool table and flops his butt on the edge, eyeing the TV, but obviously uncomfortable that his buddy Rostov has not returned. As he's facing away from me, watching the open sliding glass door, I rise and open the little bar-height door. It squeaks and he turns, and his mouth drops open as I have the M4 and it's red laser dot centered on his chest.

"You make a sound and I'll stitch your ass from your dick to your ugly snout," I say, and he's still wide-mouthed. He shuts it and nods. "Lay face down on the pool table, arms extended as far as you can reach."

He does and I lay the muzzle of the M4 against the back of his dirty blonde head and frisk him with one hand, removing the semi-auto at his side. It's a Sig-Sauer 9mm with a 13 round mag. Nice piece to add to my collection.

I glance up as someone fills the doorway of the slider, then relax as I see it's Pax.

"I wondered if you were ever gonna take the prick down," he says.

"You took care of the guy outside?"

"He's napping, hooked up to a fat bush with enough cable tie to secure a bucking bull."

I use Fitor's own pistol and crack him a good one behind the ear, and he slowly slides off the table and flops to the carpet. I grab a cable tie and bind his wrists behind his back, strip his belt away and am happy to see it's one of those web ones that will take any size, and gag him with the belt pulled so tight in his open mouth he can only barely get his breath. Then I bind his ankles and tie that cable tie to a foot of the pool table. He'll be no bother for a while.

Pax points to a hallway and we only take three steps into it before he opens a door that's glass and has an oversized bunch of grapes etched into its surface. Inside there's a small landing then a stairway going down, into what I presume is the wine cellar. The stairs are carpeted so it's quiet moving, and the door hinges are well oiled and, luckily, make no sound.

I lead the way and am pleased to see the cellar has a large open area the size of a single-car garage with a large well-lacquered slab of redwood as a table and benches on the two long sides, chairs at the end. The walls surrounding the table are floor-to-ceiling racks of wine bottles, and two wine barrels on edge are on stands at one end of the room. Bungs with spouts allow the filling of glasses.

In one of the chairs is a fat bald guy, but his head is down on his folded arms on the table and he seems to be asleep, and he's wheezing like a hippo sucking air. His baldhead is lined with veins and what I can see of his face is a mass of fine red veins. His left ear, the one I can see, is split and V-shaped through the lobe. The guy is medium height and way over medium weight...I'll bet he goes over three hun.

With his back to a post, Skip is on the floor, legs extended and spread, his head hanging, blood dripping slowly down his check and from his nose onto his bare chest. In a small separate room with its own glass door—and its walls lined with racks of bottles—stands country singer Tammy Houston, her eyes wide, blonde hair askew, her face pressed against the glass. And she's still in a yellow bikini and barefoot. And I recall they snatched her away from the pool.

I do the creep over to the sleeping fat guy, and he gets the semi-auto to the temple as did his buddy upstairs. Fat boy rolls to the side and hits the floor flat on his back, hard enough that I feel the wind from his flop.

Two pairs of cuffs hooked together bind Skip's big wrists. He's out cold, both his eyes protruding like half-eggs, and black, blue and damn near closed. I have the cuffs open in a heartbeat as I always carry a cuff key on my key chain, before he starts to stir. The first words out of his mouth are, mumbled, "Fuck you assholes. I ain't telling you shit."

I have to laugh, and reply, "I didn't ask you shit. Can you walk?"

He mumbles through busted lips. "I can run, if it means getting the hell out of here."

While I'm working on Skip, Pax is picking the keyed lock on the smaller wine room door. It opens and I guess Tammy presumes Pax is one of the good guys as he's with me; she throws her arms around him and squeezes so tight I can hear his breath expel.

Now, to get the hell out of Dodge

Target Shy & Sexy

Chapter Eighteen

I'm a little worried as so far this has been way too easy.

The good news is, as we exit the sliding glass doors, that the Dobermans are still stumbling around retching every five steps. The bad, some fat guy is standing beside them trying to figure out what the hell's wrong. Another sliding glass door, probably to the master bedroom stands open. He's not too impressive in a terry cloth robe, bare calves the size of telephone poles, fuzzy house shoes, and a prodigious belly.

He turns as we exit the sliding glass door, and yells to us, "What the hell's the matter with my boys?"

He hasn't really looked at us, and doesn't until I speak up. "Your boys are gonna be fine, and you're gonna stay alive so long as you don't make any quick moves."

Then he realizes we aren't his employees. "Who the fuck...?"

"Frick, Frack, Fred and our girl Fanny. Check the red dot in the center of your gray chest hair, old man. Sit down on your blubber butt on the grass and don't move until we're way out of sight, and you'll stay alive."

"I'm Ed Gashi, and you fuckers are dead meat."

"I know who you are, Edvin. Wrong time to act tough. That red dot on your chest could be a half dozen holes in your heart, presuming you have one."

All the time we're talking, we're moving toward the fence. Skip is stumbling along behind.

"Down," I yell at Gashi, and he complies, sitting on his butt in the grass.

But there's not a humble bone in his Albanian body, and he yells. "Dead meat, dead fucking meat."

We reach the fence, and realize it will be tough getting Tammy over it without scratching her up on the jagged fence top, so I trot back to the fat man. "Get up. Give me the robe."

"Fuck you."

"You give it or I take it off your body and I don't give a shit which."

He rolls to his side and struggles to his feet, and drops the robe off into the grass. He really is a fat fuck with rolls big enough to hide more than one weapon. I should have been more careful as there's no telling what might be hidden in the folds.

"Step back," I command, and he does.

Skip has followed me and I guess has a bone to pick with the fat Albanian. Without saying a word he snakes a hand out and grabs the man by the throat and Gashi goes up on his toes. Skip guides him, Gashi tip toeing backwards to the edge of the pool, Albanian fat quivering with every step, and shoves.

A substantial wave moves away from the hole in the water where the fat man has, in his not-so-splendid nakedness, disappeared into the water.

He bobs up and sputters, "Dead...dead...dead fucking meat. I got your ass on the security cameras, and you ain't gonna get away with this."

The dumb fuck is pointing at a camera mounted on the wall above one of the sliders, and just for the hell of it, knowing it won't destroy the tape, I raise the M4 and put a quick three round blast into the camera, blowing it all to hell. Gashi spits and treads water as both Skip and Pax yell at me.

"What the hell?"

"No problem," I yell back.

Gashi is dead silent for the moment. I grab the robe and hustle back to the fence. Pax is already on the other side. I throw the robe over, covering the jagged wires, and hoist Tammy up and he takes her down. I boost Skip up and he crashes to the soft plowed soil on the other side. I vault the fence, catch the sling on my M4, hang like a marionette, and Pax laughs. He has to help me get untangled.

"You are one clumsy fuck," he says, still laughing. "Good thing I took you to raise."

"Let's clumsy the hell out of here," I manage. Tammy's with me as the bike's lots closer. "Meet you two at the iHop in town. Don't be followed." I hand Skip the Sig-Sauer, "Thirteen in the clip and one in the chamber, a gift from the boys who roughed you up."

"10-4," he says, and they disappear into the darkness.

As I'm dragging Tammy to the bike, we can hear Gashi yelling behind us, "You're fucked. Dead meat, dead fucking meat."

I give Tammy my helmet as any gentleman would, then dig out some lightweight leathers from my saddle bags and hand them to her.

"Just the coat," she says, and pulls it on. It's way big for her but even at that only hits her to the bottom of her shapely butt.

"You'll freeze," I say.

"Not that far to town," she says, and I shrug and she climbs on and hugs me like I was the world's biggest record buyer, and we're off. I'm halfway back to town when a set of headlights roar up behind me and I'm about to see what the Harley Iron will top out at, when the red and blue lights fill my mirror.

We stop in the soft dirt of the roadside and dismount and I'm studying the white sheriff's car, my hand on the Glock at the middle of my back, but happy it's actually a sheriff's car and not Gashi and his crew. Unhappy, as I have little interest in waiting for the Albanians to regroup and give chase as I'm sure the presence of one sheriff's deputy won't stop them from trying to blow us all to hell.

He's on the radio, I hope merely reporting the stop, then dismounts and walks into his headlights, and I can see it's the same cop who jumped me in the boondocks behind Castiano Winery. Officer Brownley if memory serves, and I can see it does as he gets close and I read his nameplate.

"Where's your helmet?" he asks.

"Only had one. Gave it to the lady, like any gentleman would," I say.

He studies me a moment, trying to place me. Then looks her up and down. She's unzipped the leather jacket and shows plenty of cleavage and a well-earned gym six-pack.

Not taking his eyes off Tammy's California tan, he asks me, "Driver's license?"

I dig it out but he still doesn't tie me to the guy in the van.

He finally meets my eyes then offers, "I've got an Iron, only mine's a couple of years older and red."

"Red's good," I say, then add. "I was just giving a stranded lady a ride to town. How about you taking her in and I'll wear the helmet?"

He eyes Tammy up and down and it's plain to me he'll be happy to spend a little time with the shapely blonde, even as disheveled as she is at the moment. "Aren't you a little chilly?" he asks her, as the coat's open and her nipples are well defined.

"Freezing, can you give me that ride?"

He nods. "Jump in," he instructs her. Then turns to me. "I'd write you but I'm already off duty and am heading in to catch some breakfast...my supper...but you promise me no more riding without the helmet and I'll let it pass."

"Cross my heart. We're headed for the iHop and I'm buying."

"I can buy my own, but we'll see you there."

So far, the day is mine.

As I'm remounting the bike, my van approaches, slows but drives on past, then speeds up again. And no one is on their tail.

Brownley is a good guy, and finally relents and lets me buy breakfast. He heads out of the parking lot, happy that we're loading the Harley in the back and is gone before we pull out a new set of signs, "Coastal Beef and Poultry" and line the van with red magnetic stripes to match the red lettering on the red and blue signs. He never did make Tammy as the famous country singer she's become, but of course she's a little out of uniform.

Skip crashes in the narrow bunk in back the van and Tammy shares the passenger seat with Pax, which seems to suit him just fine. We listen to Whalen and Willy all the way back to Santa Barbara, where Pax takes over the driving duty and Tammy and I share the seat, which is just fine with me.

It's noon by the time we roll into Tammy's Malibu digs. We've called ahead, informing both Detective Howard Adamson of the LA Sheriff's Department and FBI Special Agent Robbie Quintana of the fact we've got the lady with us. Quintana questions me at some length on the cell, then does the same with Tammy, who rings off and informs us, "The FBI is getting warrants and heading to the winery. All those assholes will be in jail before the day is out."

I laugh. "Don't count on it, darling. This is not their first rodeo. They'll be long gone before the FBI can get their act together."

I have Pax call Sol, his number one guy at his ISP office in Vegas, and get him trying to get a line on Edvin Gashi and his bunch of bad boy Albanians, and he grumbles as he was in the sack, but promises to get right on it.

Adamson's plain oatmeal colored car is in Tammy's driveway and a black SUV is parked in front. Looks like we have a reception committee, which does not surprise me.

Skip is asleep and we don't wake him, but Pax, Tammy and I wander in to find Adamson, Quintana, Coogan and Tammy's friend—and now mine—beautiful long-legged Tyler at the kitchen table drinking coffee.

Tammy's head of security, Butch Horrigan, has obviously been released from UCLA Medical Center as he's flopped on her living room sofa watching the tube.

Tammy is hugged until she has to shove away from Coogan and Tyler and catch her breath. Then she runs for her bedroom.

While she's gone, I don't bother with hello, and direct my remarks to the FBI.

"I figured you'd be headed for Paso Robles and the Castiano Winery. Or isn't kidnapping still a federal crime?"

"We have two dozen agents heading there from all over the west. I've got my hands full here."

It's all I can do not to say 'full of coffee cup.' But I don't. Instead, I beg off what I'm sure will be a long Q and A session, and say, "I've got to head over to Sammy Castiano's place and settle up."

"Don't bother. It's a crime scene and full of our CSI and bomb people, and folks from the California State Attorney General's Office. It's crawling with investigators."

"Crime scene?" I ask; maybe I've misunderstood her staying here.

"You didn't have the radio on while driving back here?"

"Country western, at Tammy's request."

"Somebody blew Sammy's house into the Pacific, or at least parts of it. So far we've got six bodies."

I'm a little astounded, and stand looking perplexed for a moment. Then finally ask, "Sammy and Margo?"

"Yet to be identified, but it appears the Castianos walked in earlier this morning and weren't there fifteen minutes before the place went up like the Fourth of July. Or maybe more like Hiroshima."

I hate to be callous, but there goes one of my paydays.

Tammy returns in six inch black heels, white slacks, and a black and white polka dot silk blouse.

I'm still perplexed when Tammy's house-phone rings and Tyler answers. She turns a little white then hands the phone to Tammy.

Tammy sighs deeply, but takes it and all she says is hello, then her eyes grow wide as she turns white as well. She carefully returns the phone to the receiver.

"They said I'm next, hamburger they said, if I don't pay what Emory and what Sammy owes them…they want sixteen million."

Quintana grouses, "And I just sent the phone people home and just removed the trace."

"Doesn't matter," Pax says. "They'd be on a throwaway."

I start edging back to the door. "Let's get everyone out of here. They obviously wired Sammy's place up last night and may have done the same here. Quintana, I'd get your bomb people over here…"

"Let's get out of here," Quintana snaps, and begins to usher us all out.

"Butch!" I yell.

He doesn't answer. So I turn to Coogan, "He's your man. Get him."

"Fuck him," he says, and brushes by me.

I charge into the living room and pull the fat so-called security man to his feet, over his complaints.

"Hey, my head is still screwed—"

"Shut up, and get your ass out of here."

He doesn't argue, and allows me to lead him to the door and outside.

We make it to the curb without getting blown across the street.

Chapter Nineteen

After Quintana's people arrive, she instructs us to follow her back to her office, which is a long ride to the Federal Building on Wilshire near the 405, not far from Tammy's apartment and the scene of the original sniper act.

Tammy, still chilled to the bone, rides with Tyler and Coogan, I drive my Vette with its top down, and Pax and Skip drive the van. Which is fine as it gives us time to confer using the cell phones. Our story is Pax was not on the recovery scene at all. No reason for him to be tied up in an FBI interrogation for two days. I went in alone and snatched Skip and Tammy back. I speak to Tammy on the phone before she has a chance to relate the events to her ride chums and she agrees that Pax was nowhere to be seen at the winery. He was at the motel where I'd stashed Margo making sure no one but Sammy came to snatch her.

As we're not in custody, Pax merely drops Skip off, then he hauls ass in my van. The last thing I want is the FBI taking a hard look at my van with its hide out recesses full of weapons, most illegal, and various signs and license plates.

When we walk into the FBI western headquarters, 11000 Wilshire Boulevard, 17th Floor, Quintana immediately asks about Pax, and I inform her. "Mr. Weatherwax merely gave us some assistance by watching the location I'd stowed Mrs. Castiano. He's on his way back to work. All he knows is what the Hampton Inn looks like from the parking lot."

"Work where?" she demands.

"Las Vegas. He's got a company to run."

"Do I need to send some people to his company and place him under arrest?"

"Give his office a call. He'll drop by your Las Vegas office anytime."

"Humph," she grumbles.

We are six hours in separate interrogation rooms. Coogan finally calls one of Tammy's many attorneys, who shows up and insists he take Tammy to a physician to be checked out. I insist that Skip accompanies them as he may need a stitch or ten, and Quintana relents. And since Quintana has tickets to a Dodger's game, she kicks me out in another hour with instructions I'm to return in the morning.

However, I'm not under arrest and I am tired of answering the same questions a dozen times...so returning is not on the agenda.

We do learn that no explosives were found at Tammy's Malibu digs, that the team of agents in Paso Robles found no one other than menial employees at Castiano Winery when they raided it like Sherman storming Atlanta, and that a Cessna Citation business jet with a half dozen passengers—no flight plan filed—left the Paso airport not long after we pulled Skip and Tammy out of the wine cellar.

I call Sol and give him what I know.

All that's the good news. The bad is Tammy has a death threat.

As I'm climbing into the Vette in the Fed's parking lot, I get a call, and it's Coogan. "Tammy wants you to come to the Four Seasons to eat and figure out our next move."

"Is she okay?"

"The doc said she was fine. Your guy got a few stitches but he's fine. Maybe a slight concussion."

"You got my forty five grand."

"Yeah, asshole. I have the check in my briefcase."

"Coogan, I don't like you worth a shit, and the next time you call me anything other than Mr. Reardon, or maybe even Mike, I'm going to drag your dumb ass into the alley and teach you some manners…understand?"

He's quiet for a long count, then replies, "Tammy wants you around, so I'll put up with your dumb ass."

"Dumb ass? Is that Mr. Reardon, or Mike?"

He's silent for a moment, then mumbles. "Mike. We'll be in the dining room at the Four Seasons. She's got a room in the hotel for you and this Skip guy."

"I'm just leaving the Feds. Fifteen minutes."

The Four Seasons is on corner of South Doheny and Burton on the north edge of the commercial area of Beverly Hills, its restaurant and bar being one of the older CNBC, see-and-be-seen, classy joints in a very classy if very plastic city. More flakes than a box of Kellogg's.

Tammy, who I guess stopped at some five-grand-an-outfit Rodeo Drive shop is looking more like a million bucks in a simple black sheath, and is at a pair of tables pulled together in the bar, manager Emory Coogan on one side of her and so-called chief of security Butch Horrigan on the other. She looks like a luscious slice of sweet melon which should be flanked by prosciutto but instead is sandwiched between two suet-laden pork chops.

I really dislike both these guys. Across the table is the svelte Tyler, in a blue silk blouse and those tighter-than-skin black stretch pants clinging to her perfect curves.

I start to take a seat by Tyler, but Tammy shoos Butch away and makes room for me on her right. Coogan gives me a look like a cobra at a rat...but he moves.

Tammy pats the seat. Instead, with a bit of a Cheshire cat grin thinking he's one-upped me, Skip sits by Tyler.

As soon as I'm down, Tammy takes my cheeks in both hands and plants a wet smack right on my lips, then continues to hold my cheeks and says, "I owe you big time, Mike."

I smile. "My pleasure," then, a little on the callous side, turn to Butch on her other side. "You got a check for me?"

His jaw noticeably clinches, but he reaches down and scoops up a five hundred dollar alligator briefcase and digs around until he comes up with a check. I look him in the eye and say, "Thank you..." pause, then turn to my new boss and add, "Tammy." He goes from clinched jaw to clinched jaw with a red face.

"So," I continue, eye-to-eye with Tammy, now perfectly coiffed and made-up with slight brown eyeliner over her beautiful blue, gold speckled, eyes, "...am I officially employed as your chief of security?"

"Well," she says, with a little hesitation, "Butch here is my chief...you're on as a consultant."

I slip the check in my pocket. "I think I earned the retainer," and I rise and motion Skip to stand as well. I extend my hand to Tammy and she takes it. "Thanks, Miss Houston, but I've seen Horrigan's work and don't think I'm gonna work with him and certainly not for him. Best of luck," and I drop the hand and spin on my heel, and Skip follows me to the lobby.

"Mike," I hear Tammy yell after me, then as I make a left toward the front door, hear her high heels clicking on the marble floor. "Mike, don't go."

I hesitate and she catches up. Horrigan is close behind her and he's steaming out the ears.

"I need you," she says, pleading.

"Tammy, now that I quit I can call you Tammy, I don't suffer fools and I don't let their mistakes flow over onto me. I work with my own people, not with stumble bums like Butch here." And I nod at him, then smile as he takes a couple of quick steps my way and telegraphs a looping left. I sidestep the punch and as he stumbles by me, bury a hard right in his side, just under his rib cage, and hear him expel every ounce of breath. Then he starts to sag to his knees, but he catches himself.

So I help him with a slight sidekick just behind his left knee, and he goes down to both knees. Then, him clasping both hands to his side, I give him a small push with my boot to his back between his shoulder blades and the big boy goes to his face.

Before he can bounce, two hotel security guys are headed my way. I hold up both hands, palm out, and probably because Skip is beside me, man-mountain himself, they stop six feet from us. "What's going on here?" the larger of the two asks.

"All over, sir." I say, giving him a smile, then add, "Butch here took offense at something I said, but he's decided not to object further."

"Take it outside, fellas, and down the block away from the hotel."

"No problem," I say, then turn to Tammy. "See what I mean. Get yourself some help who'll keep you alive," and again head for the door.

"Mike," she calls after me, "you're head of security."

Target Shy & Sexy

Chapter Twenty

I stop and turn back slowly. The two security guys are helping Butch to his feet. I cross back to where Tammy stands and suggest in my most sincere tone, "Don't say it unless you mean it, Tammy."

"I mean it," she reiterates.

"Then it's Miss Houston, since I'm working for you again."

She shrugs.

I move over to where the two security guys are brushing Butch off like he might sue the joint if he's not treated with deference. "Butch," I say, getting his undivided attention as well as that of the two guys flanking him. "You're fired."

"What the fuck," he says, but does not even consider trying another cheap shot. Instead he turns to Tammy and repeats, "What the fuck?"

Tammy merely shrugs, "Mike's the head of security," then she heads back to the bar. Coogan has come as far as the door between bar and lobby, and doesn't look happy as his jaw is still clamped and his face red. He spins on his heel and leads Tammy back to the table.

Skip and I follow, but when she sits I move to her side and say in a low tone. "Skip and I are two tables away and will stay separate from you. It's best."

"Okay," she says.

"Advise me when you're ready to leave so one of us can lead, and one follow. Okay?"

"10-4," she says, and I have to smile.

As I move to a nearby table, the hotel manager—or so his nameplate says—strides into the bar and to her table. He's a distinguished looking guy wearing a dark gray suit with light gray pinstripes, a gray cufflink shirt, and a gray and yellow power tie. He looks great except for the bed-head doo. Why a guy would have a perfect shine on Gucci loafers on one end, and a mess on the other is a little beyond my ken.

"Miss Houston, is there a problem?" he asks, with an English accent that sounds a little contrived.

"Not now."

"We can't have—"

She stops him short. "We haven't occupied my suite or the other rooms yet. If you prefer, we'll head over to the London or St. James?"

His manner changes immediately. "No, no, so long as the drama is over."

She smiles demurely, and he spins on his heel. "Drinks are on the hotel," he says.

"Thank you," Tammy calls after him. I guess the four or five grand a night yields some influence, even at the Four Seasons.

We grab a great supper in the dining room, Tammy miffed because we refuse to sit with her and Coogan, taking a nearby table where we can watch the door and her six.

Coogan leaves after downing his dessert, a mound of chocolate syrup covered something, and doesn't bother to say goodnight. My info on him tells me he has a house in Brentwood and I presume he's headed there. Tammy signs the ticket, walks over and sits with Skip and me, and I shake my head.

"Tammy, you don't get it. We don't want to broadcast that we're part of your entourage. It puts you in extra danger and puts us in extra danger. You've got to remember, at all times, you're a target...as sweet and sexy as you are and as incongruous as it seems, you're a target."

She pouts, but nods. "Okay, okay, it's time to go up."

I give a high sign to Skip and he takes the lead. Only after he's had a chance to check out the entry, lobby and elevators, I escort Tammy out.

She has a rooftop suite large enough for her and her band, and has gotten us rooms on the floor below as the other suite on the floor is taken.

The elevator stops a floor below hers, and I have to object. "Won't do, Miss Houston. We need to be nearby, not an elevator ride away."

She giggles, showing the effects of the several champagne cocktails she's had with her fillet. "Then I guess you'll just have to share the suite with me."

"There are two doubles in the second bedroom?"

"There are."

"Then both Skip and I will share the suite with you...and would even if we had to sleep on the floor."

"Reardon," she asks, with a coquettish look, pressing the close door button, "are you afraid of me?"

"I only fear God and the IRS," I say, with a laugh. "Skip and I will take the second bedroom. Why don't you call the desk and try to get your money back for the unused rooms."

"Whatever," she says, sounding a little disgusted. We enter the suite and Skip steps in front of her. He goes to the master bedroom and clears it, the deck outside it, and the bathroom, then returns and gives me a nod.

"Goodnight, Miss Houston," I say, and she gives me a wave over her shoulder and disappears into her half of the suite.

Skip always has trouble sleeping so he tunes in the living room TV to an old movie and I hit the sack. I have trouble sleeping late so at four thirty, I get up and shower, luxuriating for a long time, then shave—the suite has every amenity—and go out and wake Skip, who's asleep on the sofa.

"Go get some decent rest. I'll catch the news and wake you when I hear the lady stirring."

Luckily the suite has the makings for coffee in its small kitchen, and I'm on my fourth cup and fifth news channel when my phone rings with an unknown caller.

"Reardon," I answer.

"Mike, it's Crystal Janson." Crystal is the twin sister of a client of mine, Carol, who was killed by the cartel, and is raising Carol's daughter, her niece, Sherry. I haven't heard from her in months and smile at the sound of her voice. Her salon, Beauty by Crystal, is only a few blocks from Pax's building in Vegas.

"How are you? How's Sherry?"

"She's fine. Have you heard?"

I can see this is not a pleasure call. "Heard what?"

"Your buddy, Pax what's his name…his office had an explosion."

That knocks the wind out of me. "When?"

"Not more than a half hour ago. I guess there were a half-dozen workers there."

"Bad?"

"Very bad, blew the whole front of the building off."

"I gotta go. I'll come see you soon. Thanks for the call."

I immediately dial Pax and get call forwarding to an answering device. Then I try Sol and get the same. I don't bother trying the office phone. Instead I dial a friend at LVDP, and he picks up.

"Bollinger," he answers.

"Andre, Mike Reardon here. I just heard there was an explosion at Weatherwax Internet."

"Yeah, your buddy as I recall."

"What's the story?"

"I'm there now. They've got the fire out and have recovered two bodies and hauled four out and have bussed them to emergency at University Medical Center...UMC."

"And Pax?"

"Don't know what's up with individual names yet."

"Can you call me on this cell number when you do?"

"Sure. You'll owe me."

"I already owe you."

I hustle in and wake Skip. "The ka ka's hit the fan in Vegas. Explosion at Pax's office, he doesn't answer, and I can't find out shit. I'm driving over in the van. Don't let Tammy do anything stupid, stay close to her."

"Got it," he says, wiping the sleep from his eyes.

"Follow me down to the van and I'll leave you with a duffle bag full of goodies."

He jumps up and drags on his clothes. "Call me as soon as you know what's up. After driving over half of Iraq in a lousy Humvee, it would be the worst if Pax bought it from an explosion in Vegas."

"Get ready to get a phone call telling you to shag to Vegas. I think this has to be our Albanian friends, and I'm going to rock their world as soon as I know what's what. If we finish them, we'll finish the threat to Tammy."

"And Tammy in the meantime?" he asks as we head for the door.

"I've got a couple of buddies here in LA and will get you some help."

"I'll take care of this end until I hear from you...you take care of Vegas."

And we are soon at valet parking and then in my van. I drive to a side parking space and Skip and I fill a duffle full of whatever he might need to watch out for our client, and I'm gone.

I'm happy when I reach Killer Carlos Juarez on the first try, and he agrees to head for the Four Seasons and tie up with Skip. And he's got a buddy, Tobin "To Bad" Michaels, who'll work the job. I've heard tales of Michaels, a real bad ass. Both of these guys are ex-Green Berets, now bail enforcement agents, a little older than me but not too long in the tooth for this kind of work.

Before I make the turn north out of San Berdo thru Cajon Pass, my phone rings and I use the hands-free.

"Reardon."

It's Andre. "Weatherwax is alive...in the operating room. He was in his office on top in the back of the building. He's hurt pretty bad as the floor collapsed and some crap landed on him. The receptionist is dead as some asshole backed a pickup through the glass wall in front, right in front of her desk, and ran for it. If our guy's guess is right, the pickup was loaded with nitrogen fertilizer soaked in diesel fuel and blew the whole building to hell and took out half the adjoining buildings."

"The receptionist. Rosie Newmyer?"

"That's the lady."

"And the kid, Sol Goldman?"

"Not one of the dead. Three confirmed dead now. Two walked away with scratches and bruises, unable to hear, but they walked away. The receptionist and another lady and a young guy are at the morgue."

"Those dirty motherfuckers." I have a ball of snakes in my belly, a throat dry as the Gobi, and my jaw's clamped so tight it'll be sore for a week. Rosie was a great girl, chubby, happy, always with a grin and a giggle. I'm developing a knot of reptiles in my stomach so tight that it feels a little like a bowling ball, and I know it won't dissolve until I put whoever did this toes up. Hopefully after them hurting for a good long spell before their lights go out.

"You know who did this?" Andre snaps, now all cop.

"I have an idea. I'm heading over Cajon pass. I'll see you in three hours or so."

"I'll still be at the scene. We've got a team from the FBI bomb squad coming in. We're stretching it but I appealed to them as I said I had reason to believe it was a terrorist act. But if you think you know who did it, I can get a jump on taking them down."

"You may not be too far wrong. I'll bring you up to speed when I get there."

"Reardon…no cowboy crap."

"Yippee-ki-yay." I say.

I hear him sigh deeply, then he says. "See you at…a little before noon?"

"I'll head for the hospital first. Call me again if you get any more news."

"Reardon, don't fuck up my town again."

"Nothing but self-defense, detective. You know that."

Target Shy & Sexy

Chapter Twenty-One

Just as I reach Barstow, I get another unidentified caller, and use the hands-free.

"Reardon."

"Mike, did you hear?" And I recognize Sol's voice, Pax's number one man and my little buddy who I've been worrying about.

"I did. Good to hear your voice. You okay?"

"I was across town working on a client's server. This is terrible, just terrible."

"And you are just the guy to help me kick some ass."

"I don't do guns, Mike."

"It's not guns I need. What have you found out about these Albanian assholes?"

"Five of them flew into McCarran last night, along with two big dogs. I tapped the video cameras at the fixed base operator they use. Then, figuring where they were probably headed, the security system at the casino. They all went directly to Rocco's Casino out in Laughlin. Word is Rocco's is really owned by this Edvin Gashi and Armand Ahmeti, and Rodolfo 'Rocco' Barbini is merely a front so they could get by the gaming commission."

"Get a take on how many Albanians are hanging out there, and who lives at the club. Going in from Henderson Rocco's is the second one on the river side, right?"

"Yes. I'll have to work out of my apartment. I hate to leave the hospital until I know what's up with Pax and a couple of my buddies, Fletcher and Bohannan, who are hurt bad too."

"Let's get these assholes. That's the best thing we can do for Pax and your pals."

"Got it. I'm headed home."

The phone doesn't rattle again and I drive straight to the University Medical Center. I'm happy to find out that Pax is in a room and not Intensive Care. Visitor's hours are not until mid-afternoon, unless you're family…but if I'm not family no one is.

It's a private room and when I peek in the door, I see he's flat on his back and staring out the window, his good leg tilted up in traction, his right arm in a cast, and a couple of IVs in the back of his left hand. I wander on in.

"Wanna race?" I ask.

"Speak up. My ears are still ringing from the explosion. Yeah, I wanna race…to find out who tried to wipe us all out."

"I've got a good idea. It didn't take Gashi long to nail you from his security video and to put his scumbag boys to work."

"You sure it was him?"

"Sure enough. Sol…thank God Sol was gone…tracked them back to McCarran early this morning and we know they're out at Rocco's in Laughlin. I've got him doing some recon so we can play get even."

"I want to be in on it," Pax says, and I laugh.

"You wanna wait six weeks. Hell, they'll likely be out of the country in less than a week. The FBI hit the winery already, and they were long gone back here. I've got some help."

He looks out the window again, staring at nothing, then turns back to me, "Patty Yount was a single mother with a five year old daughter. Rosie has…had…two kids and her disabled mom lived with her. Betty Polkinghorn was the sole support for her niece after her sister OD'd last year. Donald McDowel has…had…a pregnant wife. I want every one of those Albanian pricks to be catfish crap at the bottom of Lake Mead."

"You know I loved Rosie like a sister...and I know all of them were good folks. I'll get the pricks, but we'd better not wait for you to get well or they'll fly the coop."

"You're right. Get those assholes. I'll owe you big time," Pax says, then coughs until I think he's about to spit up a lung. I'm about to call for a nurse, when he gets it under control. Then he explains, "I laid in a pile of timber, plaster, roofing, and equipment while the fire started to roar. I breathed some bad crap. I thought I was cooked, then the fire boys knocked it down and jacked some debris up and got me out. I breathed some really, really bad crap. I'm afraid some of my people died hard."

"You're too tough to cook. Are they gonna have them take an inch out of that busted good leg of yours so you won't walk in circles?"

"Fuck you. I'm tired and I can't hear but about half of your bullshit. Get the hell out of here."

"Just so you know I know…it was my job that brought this down on you, and I'm gonna make it right."

"Mike, I guess you didn't hear me. Get the hell out of here."

"I'm not leaving until we've got someone good on your door, twenty-four-seven."

"Whatever," he says, and closes his eyes. Then he whispers, barely loud enough to hear. "When the fuck did we start keeping score?"

"Yeah, yeah," I say back, then I wander out in the hall and call Detective Andre Bollenger. "I need someone on the door at Weatherwax's room. These boys seem to want him pretty bad."

"Reardon, the Las Vegas Metro Police are not your personal protection agency. I can get someone, off duty, in uniform—"

"Twenty-four-seven."

"—Twenty-four-seven will mean three guys. That'll cost you two hun a shift or six hun a day. Cash, to them personally. They need the dough."

"When can you get someone here? Someone good. And well-armed."

"An hour or two."

"Anything new from the scene?"

"The pickup was stolen, of course. We've got some video of a guy running past the bank a couple of doors down."

"When can I see it?"

"Meet me at my office at six and we'll take a look. And you can tell me who you think is responsible."

"Six," I say, without promising.

Someone is trying to call as I'm hanging up and I switch over and answer.

"I got some interesting stuff," Sol says.

"I'm waiting here for some guys to guard Pax's room then I'll come your way. Text me an address. It may be a couple of hours."

"I'll keep churning the computer." I can hear the smile in his voice. "They got toilet paper for firewalls."

I wish I had time to drive to Laughlin, but it's about ninety miles. Instead I'm stuck here. It's only forty-five minutes before a square-jawed black officer who looks like he should be playing tackle for the 49ers shows up. I can see he's wearing a vest and has a combat shotgun as well as his sidearm. It seems

Andre is taking things seriously, and I relax a little. The cop says he'll be on the job until twelve thirty, then another off-duty cop will pick up the baton until eight thirty, then a third until four thirty and they'll start all over.

And I'm off to Sol's apartment, which is only about six blocks east of the hospital. He doesn't live fancy, except for the computer and stereo equipment. He's got a sound system that might just knock the walls down...walls covered with posters of Katy Perry, Shakira, and Jessie James. I'd guess him to be a real music fan but none of the ladies have on enough clothes to cover a pocket size MP3 player. Maybe music is second on the list with Sol.

I have my Mac Air laptop under my arm.

"There's a beer in the fridge," he announces after I let myself in.

"Working." I refuse.

"I've emailed you a pile of crap. I've got reams of stuff on the Albanians and on Rocco's, including plans and specs and am tapped into their security system. We see what they see, real time."

"Cool. How many of them are hanging out there?"

"They have two suites, Gashi and Ahmeti, and five rooms with guys doubled up in them...but Gashi and four of their guns are gone. They flew out of McCarran a half hour ago. They got other security guys on the job, but I think they're run-of-the-mill locals."

"Flew? Where to?"

"I haven't pegged it yet. I'm trying to get into Burton Aviation's server now. The Citation they've been chartering belongs to Burton. If I don't get the info there I'll go after a flight plan."

"Keep working, I'll read."

In minutes while I'm studying the layout for Rocco's, Sol slams a hand down on his mouse pad.

"Damn, damn, they're headed out of the country."

"I'm not surprised." Maybe I will have to clue in Andre and the FBI, to get them stopped before they reach the border. "Where?" I ask.

"Vera Cruz, Mexico, if it's a real flight plan, which I doubt...so God knows where."

"Are they out of the country?"

Sol glances at his watch. "If they're not, they will be in a few minutes if they're headed due south. We're screwed."

"Then those five are down the list somewhere. I'll take care of them later, if I have to go to Albania to do it. Who's left at Rocco's?"

"What are you going to do?" Sol asks.

"Pardner, you don't want to know. As soon as we're done here you're going on vacation."

He glares at me. "Bullshit, Mike. They were my friends too. Whatever you're gonna do, I'm gonna help you do. Final word."

I can't help but smile. Then I suggest, "I don't think you'd do too well in the big house, Sol. You'd be fresh meat for some ugly ol' boys."

"Fuck it. I'm in."

I shrug. "Then let's go to work."

Chapter Twenty-Two

We work in Sol's apartment for over an hour, doing recon on Rocco's Casino and Resort and the unincorporated town of Laughlin, Nevada, which is on the Colorado River not far from Arizona's Bullhead City on the other side. The town is still on its butt after the recession of 2008, not having recovered like Vegas did. Ten primary resorts and casinos make up by far the biggest employers in Laughlin, with only seven thousand five hundred residents.

Rocco's is nowhere near the largest. The Tropicana has fifteen hundred rooms and a huge casino floor, and employees account for almost ten percent of the population of Laughlin. Rocco's has two hundred rooms and a casino floor of only a little over twelve thousand square feet, eighty feet by one thirty. Where the Trop has a huge showroom Rocco's holds only three hundred, and best we can figure, has only a few over one hundred employees.

Sol has gotten into Rocco's servers with little problem, and we have photos and physical descriptions of all the Albanians living there, even though they are not officially employees—they certainly wouldn't pass roster with the gaming commission—they do have photo ID tags and those photos are still in the server, simply deleted by someone who thinks that removes them from the system. I presume they had badges made so they can move unchallenged throughout the property.

We're able to identify two of the hotel rooms vacated that had been occupied for many months by four of those Albanians. I presume those are four of the five who've accompanied Gashi out of the country. One guy must have been rooming with someone who didn't go.

That meant that at least five, and maybe six guns remained at Rocco's with Ahmeti, Gashi's partner. They must have figured that since the FBI was after Gashi due to Tammy's kidnapping, and now possibly due to the bombing and murder of the Castiano's and their employees, and soon, likely due to the bombing of Weatherwax Internet Services, it was propitious to get the hell out of Dodge.

It's time for me to meet with Detective Andre Bollenger and take a look at the video of the pickup driver. I pause at the door and ask Sol one more time. "Are you sure you want to be a part of this?"

I wouldn't have believed Sol was capable of a hard look, but he's giving me one. "I said, final word, and I mean just that."

"Sol, these guys cost Pax lots of dough and damn near killed the best friend I've ever had. They killed a good friend, Rosie, and created a bunch of orphans and dependents. I'm gonna take these guys down, but I'm also going to take every dime of theirs I can get my hands on. You'll make some dough as will every guy who takes the risk with me, but by far the most of it will go to a few kids, a disabled grandma, and whoever got screwed by these guys. Is that agreeable?"

"Pax pays me good. Whatever the deal is, I'm in."

I like the kid because he's good at what he does and works his dick in the dirt, and now I like him even more.

Andre's office is on the second floor, and I'm not in a mood to wait for an elevator. He's at his desk in an end of hall office and sees me coming, and is up and out the door, waving me to follow. He turns into a conference room with a screen and one of those small digital projectors on the table, and without so much as a hello, starts the video.

I flop down in a chair and watch a couple of housewives tap the ATM, then a guy who looks like Tom Cruise except he's way too tall makes a deposit, then flattens himself next to the ATM as a guy hauls ass by at a dead run.

"Can you stop this thing?" I ask, and Andre jumps the disk backwards, runs it a second, and stops it.

I can clearly see it's the guy called Fitor, with the dirty blonde hair and pockmarked face, but I shrug. "Can't be positive."

Andre looks disgusted. "How about a guess?"

"You know how these IDs are, particularly on video—"

"You said you have an idea who might have done this."

"Andre, I said an idea. I'm not sure."

"Reardon, you're dicking me around. You don't want us to get in the way of whatever you've got in your black little heart. I don't want you shooting up the town…again. So spit it up. Who do you think pulled this off?"

"Andre, if I were even half sure, I'd speak up, but I'm not."

"I saw your jaw knot when you got a good look at this runner. You know who he is."

"When I know for sure, I'll call."

"Get the fuck out of here. Friend or not, I'm gonna bust your ass if you do your cowboy crap again."

"When I know for sure, I'll call."

He points to the door, and I head out, calling behind me, "Thanks for the show."

157

"Yeah, and we got flat screens in the jail now. Why do I get the feeling that's where you're headed?"

I wave over my shoulder, and am gone. I'm halfway back to Sol's apartment when my iPhone jingles out an unknown caller ring, and I answer, "Reardon."

"I got some good stuff," Sol reports.

"Give me twenty minutes."

"It's supper time. You buying the pizza and beer?"

"You got some good stuff and I'm buying a steak."

"How about where some guys are meeting up to split up eight figures of cash tomorrow night?"

"Foreign guys."

"Hell, I can't say half their names."

"Be out in front and I'll pick you up."

As soon as I hang up, I call Skip.

"Hey, man," he answers, "How's the Paxman?"

"Healing. Killer Carlos and Tobin show?"

"They did, and they know their stuff. But you're on the shitlist."

"With Tammy…how soon they forget."

"She called you a few names and said she wished you were here so she could fire you in person."

"I'll be a while, and she'll probably fire us both because I need you here tomorrow."

"There goes my new head of security job."

"Shit happens."

"I got no wheels."

"Cab it to Burbank, get the first flight out and I'll pick you up, either McCarran or Laughlin. Whichever you can get to the quickest."

"10-4. I'll call when I got a seat. I'll have to leave the duffle bag with these boys."

"Good. And tell Killer I'm depending upon him."

"10-4."

Now to see just what good ol', or should I say, good young Sol has pried out of hyperspace.

Target Shy & Sexy

Chapter Twenty-Three

Sol, who's a bit of a health nut, has talked me into P.F. Chang's rather than a steak house, which suits me fine. He's halfway through a whole rock cod on a bed of braised vegetables and I'm well into some delicious Peking duck by the time he's told me the whole story. He pulled a series of emails, none more than hours old, between Edvin Gashi and Armand Ahmeti. They were encrypted and in code so he spent two hours making sense of them.

It seems the conclusion is that Gashi has to stay on the run and he was only able to scrape a little over two million off the count tables at Rocco's, and wants twelve million more...what he says is a fair figure to buy him out of his half of Rocco's. Which means at least twelve million bucks will be transported tomorrow, from Rocco's in Laughlin to the meeting place at a small airport in Quartzsite, Arizona. It seems Gashi doesn't want to be seen anywhere near Vegas or even Laughlin, which I hope means he's coming personally.

The boys have traded some harsh words, even threats, via email as it seems Ahmeti was against making the loan to Castiano in the first place even though he did want to own Castiano's road construction company, then against kidnapping Tammy to try and extort the dough out of her, then adamantly against both bombings—which makes me reconsider turning Ahmeti toes up. However, as part of settling with Gashi for the price he did, I learn Ahmeti's promised to finish off a couple of guys by the name of Weatherwax and Reardon, and some big blonde guy who they've yet to ID.

One should never telegraph one's punches, even via email. Ahmeti's back to number two on my dance card.

The good news is my plan was to hit Rocco's and clean out the count room, and I had a pretty good idea how to do it after studying the plans and seeing that a six-foot by eight-foot pipe tunnel runs under the count room, but now all I have to do is knock over a vehicle transporting a pile of money…and if a few Albanian guys meet their maker in the process, all the better.

But my first course of action is to see that Pax and his people are made as right as can be made by money.

We don't have a lot of time to come up with a plan. And I don't have nearly enough in the way of troops. One, in fact, who knows how to wield the weapons that will undoubtedly be necessary.

It's the Viking and me, and probably at least a half-dozen guns on their side.

Now if Gashi only shows up to pick up his dough, and if Ahmeti himself delivers.

I look up the Quartzsite airport on my iPhone while we're eating and see it's only eight hundred feet elevation but only two thousand feet in length. I also look up the requirements for a Cessna Citation CJ4, which is the aircraft they've been chartering. The airstrip can't handle the Citation, so now the question is, will Gashi risk a trip back into the states in some small prop plane? Or will he trust one of his crumb-bums to transport millions? I've already made up my mind that I'll follow him to hell and back, should he not show up.

He's a dead man so long as I have a breath.

Driving directions tells me it's ninety miles to Laughlin and another one twenty-five to Quartzrite. So we've got two hundred and fifteen miles to figure out where to take down the boys and their dough.

And I've got a couple of ideas about how to get it done. While Sol is ruining his health with some gooey dessert—after claiming to be a healthnut—I give an old friend a call. Hector Bohannan was a master sergeant and served in Desert Storm, his last duty station, when Pax and I did. Like both of us, he ended up in Vegas and as he was a ground supply expert he took a job with a large equipment rental concern. The owner, Bobby Howard Beuford, BoHo to his friends, was an Alabama boy and an ex-member of the KKK, and Bohannan, Bojangles as he was called by those of us who served with him, is big, black—however, in the Corps, we're all green—and like most Corps master sergeants, takes no shit from no one. For some unknown reason the two of them bonded, and when Beuford died of a heart attack, sans heirs, Hector found himself in his will and owning BHB Equipment, a couple of million bucks worth of rental business.

And even at eight PM, Bojangles answers his business line—I heard it click over to call forwarding—on the second ring.

"You can't afford a secretary, or what?" I ask without bothering with hello.

"I do believe I recognize this po' old broken down voice as that of drummed out of the Corps candy ass Mike Reardon. Wha's up, easy money?"

"I'll go for all of that except candy ass. I can still take you two out of three falls."

163

"You and the rest of your squad maybe."

"How the hell are you, Bojangles?"

"Still shakin' it. You ain't calling me to check on my health, bro, so what's up?"

"I need a flat bed, a dozen of those big old orange and yellow barrels they use on the highway to divert traffic, a trailer behind the truck with a skip loader aboard—if that's the way you haul 'em—a dump truck, and one of those programmable signs to tell traffic what's up down the road."

"Oh, shit. Who's day are you gonna ruin now...and do you have a driver's license so's we can execute a legitimate rental agreement?"

"Since when do you and I need an agreement, legit or not?"

"Since I knows you're probably gonna fuck everything up and my insurance won't be worth dog doo unless I gots an agreement. And I guess you gots cash to pay up front?"

"I got a license. I got cash. Dick Strong from Tallahassee, Florida."

"I don't give a damn if it's George Clooney from Hollywood, so long as it passes muster and you sign the name on the license on my rental agreement so's my insurance is good to go."

"I can be at your yard in thirty minutes. You got security cameras?"

"Sure."

"Then I'll be disguised a wee bit. Don't let it bother you."

"Unless you come as Beelzebub, it don't mean squat."

"I'll be a little ugly, not that ugly. I need to hire a couple of guys, who meet your standards, five hundred each for the next twenty-four hours. Guys who can operate the equipment. And they gotta go with the gear in an hour or so."

"You gonna get them shot?"

"No, but they gotta be able to keep their mouths shut."

"I got a couple of guys who need the work. But they are good guys and I don't want them to get hurt or end up in the joint."

"Make it a grand a day and so long as they do their job, they won't get hurt or crossways with the law."

"Your word is good enough for me. Now I gotta go explain to the big boss why I gotta go back to work."

"Do it, and tell Aletha I still love her."

"You ain't big enough or near black enough for my mama to love you back, so don't get your hopes up."

"Tell her anyway."

"I will, bro, see you in a half hour."

With a buddy in Hollywood who's into special effects, I'm well stocked with disguises. I've got a cigar size box in my van with a bill cap with plastic props that flare my ears until I look a little like Dumbo, with nostril inserts that make my nose as wide as Bojangles, and with cheek inserts making me look a little like the Godfather. It's enough to screw up facial recognition software and right before I get to BHB I pull into a mini-market to fill the tank, then take the time to rearrange my face.

I conclude my business with Bojangles and return to Sol's place while the boys, Frank Pattison and Dallas McQueen, who I've hired, wait in the parking lot in the trucks. If the way they loaded the truck is any example, and the calluses on their hands an indicator, both of them know how to get a job done. And the best news, they ask no questions.

Sol's assignment is to track the Albanians and keep me apprised of their movements. It's a little over a three-hour drive from Laughlin to Quartzsite, and their meeting with the other half of the Albanian contingency is set up for six PM, which means they'll have to leave by 2:30 or so.

Luckily, as I'm heading back to the parking lot, my phone rings with the Theme from Odin. It's Skip.

"I'll be in Laughlin in an hour and a half."

"It'll take me at least that long to get there, in fact I'll be at least a half hour late as I've got to go to the mini-storage. Be at the curb in two hours. We've got lots of work to do tonight."

"10-4."

I pick a spot to meet Frank and Dallas and head for the mini-storage to stock the van with any of my weapons and tricks I might need, and am off to try and make things as right as I can.

And it may just take all the tricks I know, to do so.

With Sol on his way to Laughlin to keep track of the Albanians, I'm on my way to pick up Skip. I question if two of us are enough, but two's what it's gonna be.

We need to do a recon of the site, and it's gotta be by eyeballs. Even Google Earth won't suffice.

We're a convoy. Skip and I in the van, the flatbed loaded with the big rubber barrels and the lighted highway information sign towing a trailer loaded with a skip loader, and the dump truck. I let Skip take the wheel of the van so I can catch an hour of zees in the cot in the back of the van—cramped as the Harley Iron shares the space—and Frank Pattison is on the wheel of the flatbed and Dallas McQueen is driving the dump truck. Bojangles assured me they were expert with the operation of the sign and the skip loader.

We're all gonna have to be very, very good at what we do.

Chapter Twenty-Four

The fastest route from Laughlin takes you south into California for a while, down to Needles, California where you pick up Highway I-40, then onto US95 south toward Parker, Arizona, then south the Blythe, and on south to Quartzsite. You're in three states during the short trip. Basically following the Colorado River as it meanders to Mexico.

But I don't plan to go as far as the third state.

Before you get to Parker, while still in California, I happen to know just the right spot to handle the heist and dispatch the Albanians—with luck, Fitor and his boss Ahmeti, in California. Then, hopefully, onto the Quartzsite airport and Gashi, if he shows.

Vidal Junction will do just fine.

Knowing there's a California Highway Patrolman who hangs out at Vidal Junction, the site of an inspection station, we've got to be careful. But I know the area and that's a great big advantage.

I've been there before, where I started a fight between a dozen or more cartel guys who ended up doing most of my work for me as they thought they were mad at each other, thanks to Pax's machinations on Photoshop and the computer.

Highway 95 is a two-lane road, with a few tight spots that'll be easy to block...or should I say easy to detour the traffic with a nearly phony blockage. And just before that tight spot is a turn off to an abandoned talc mine. And the road there, at least the first half mile even though gravel, looks good enough to serve as a detour.

We recon the tight spot then I show Frank and Dallas a good place to get off the road and unload the skip loader so they can fill the dump truck. Then another spot where they can park the dump truck just beyond where they'll block the road. It's critical that things go like clockwork as this is a highway and blocking it for long will be a cluster fuck that's untenable and worse, one that will be difficult from which to escape. Needless to say, it will attract the California Highway Patrol who might take umbrage if there's a gun battle going on nearby.

While Skip and I recon the gravel road to the mine, Frank and Dallas load the dump truck then program the trailered LED highway sign.

We've got lots of time as all of this is done by mid-morning. Vidal Junction is a wide spot in the road, with an inspection station operated by the State of California, a gasoline service station, and a gas and diesel truck stop with cafe and small motel. So we head for the cafe to fuel the body as Skip and I have no idea how long it will be before we chow down again.

The hell of it is I can never eat much when I have an op staring me in the face, particularly an op where the other side has all the odds. They've got the numbers, but we've probably got the firepower with some trick electronics, fully automatic weapons, a sniper rifle that either Skip and I are better than average with—Pax is the expert and I wish he were on it—and an RPG in case things get really serious. But I don't want to use it as paper money burns, and with luck the van will be chock-full.

Skip has no problem with chow and while I fight my way through a couple of eggs, a side of bacon, and a piece of wheat toast, he dusts off biscuits and gravy, a chicken fried steak that covers the plate, three eggs, and a short stack. I'm surprised he can walk but am not surprised when he suggests, "We've got a few hours so let's head back to the road to the mine so I can catch some zees."

I laugh. "Okay." Then I turn to Dallas and Frank. "You guys have some reading material or a deck of cards?"

Dallas was the talkative one. "I brought a Playboy and a Sports Afield. We're good to go."

"I'll call you and give you at least an hour's notice."

"Yeah, we got it."

So we head back.

The road to the mine is flanked by small hills and some small ravines cross it, some edged with mesquite, some with smoke trees, and one small hill crowned by a pair of cottonwoods. From the cottonwoods it's only a hundred yards to where I plan to stop the Albanians.

One of my favorite gadgets is a black Parrot Jumping Sumo Bluetooth Robot Insect Mini Drone, a mouthful of a name for a device that's only about fourteen inches wide at the wheel base and about eight inches tall, which is at first glance a little more than a video camera mounted between two wheels but in fact is much more. It's radio controlled, will actually jump obstacles, and will move at over six feet a second.

I find a spot under a greasewood bush, a spot where it has easy access to the road, and top it with a fist sized gob of Semtex and insert a telephone activated detonator. It's now a bomb that can see and crawl, in fact run and jump.

For a couple of hundred bucks I have a device that the Corps would likely pay a couple of hundred thousand for, if it were created for the defense industry. The second Insect Mini Drone I hide under a sagebrush, with equal easy access, forty feet down the road from the first, just in case the Albanians come in two vehicles, and even if not it'll be a backup bomb.

The third is merely an observation device.

You can't have too many eyes on the enemy.

It's a quadcopter with a GoPro video camera mounted thereon, and unlike the last one I owned, this one has a Bluetooth program that allows the operator to see on his iPhone in real time. It, too, is radio-controlled, via an iPhone app, as is the camera. She's fast, can fly high, can hover, and can record all she sees as well as transmit in real time. A hell of a device for chump change.

We're only two guys, but two guys armed like two dozen, and with mechanical eyes that don't care if they get in harm's way.

My phone jingles with and unknown caller and I answer.

"Reardon."

"They're driving out, Mike. They loaded a van with four large suitcases and other cases large enough to hold rifles. Ahmeti and another guy, a blonde guy who might be that Fitor guy, got in a black Cadillac and led out. Four guys are in the van."

It's just after noon, so they're leaving early. "Okay, are you following?"

"Yep, I'm staying back a block or so until we clear town, then I plan to give them at least a half mile...like you said."

"Pay close attention. When you're fifteen miles out of needles...watch your odometer...call me. Keep an eye on the other traffic and tell me how many cars or trucks are nearby. When you've gone another ten miles, turn around and haul ass back to Vegas. You don't want to be close when this comes down. You got it?"

"I got it, I don't like it—"

"Sol, I may need lots more help from you and you can't help Pax, or me, or all those kids without parents if you're coyote food out here in this God-forsaken desert. Got it?"

"I got it."

"Swear on your mother's life?"

"My mom died in a bombing in Israel three years ago."

"The hell you say. I'm sorry. Okay, swear on her memory."

"Okay, okay, I get it."

"Swear."

"I swear, I swear. Ten more miles then I turn around."

"Call me fifteen miles out of Needles."

"10-4."

"That-a-boy."

The van is parked over the hill with the cottonwoods on top—the desert around the mine is lined with two track roads—and I've unloaded the Harley Iron in case Skip and I need to go in different directions. We have belt clipped radios with the latest in wireless ear buds, and hands-free microphones. And we've both put on Kevlar vests and battle rattle belts, each with a pair of fragmentation grenades, and four extra thirty round clips for the M4's we carry. We flip for who's to man the .308 as we're both about equal in its use. I win, so I set up at the base of the cottonwoods.

And now it's the hard part. Wait.

Target Shy & Sexy

Chapter Twenty-Five

I t's just after one thirty PM when my phone jingles.

I answer. "Reardon."

"Mike, I'm coming up on the fifteen mile mark. There's a brown UPS truck, a semi, about a mile or maybe a mile and a half in front of the Cadillac, the white van is a hundred yards back of the Cad. There's a couple of SUVs in front of the UPS truck if nothing's changed. Red one and a tan one, I think. These guys don't seem to be in a hurry as they've been driving the speed limit."

"Okay, if anything changes, call me again. Remember, ten more miles then you haul ass."

As soon as he's off I call Dallas. "You've got couple of SUVs, a red one and a tan one my guy thinks, then a brown UPS truck that's your go sign. As soon as you see him coming get ready to light up the detour sign and one of you roll out the barrels while the other dumps the truckload in the road the instant the UPS guy passes. You gotta move quick as you've only got a minute or so."

"Good luck, Reardon," Dallas says, and hangs up.

Skip was set up on on the far side of the road, up a slope where he was concealed behind a pile of boulders. In less than ten minutes, my phone chimes

"Yeah."

"I can see the brown truck. We're a minute out. Good luck."

"Don't let any other vehicle follow them. Block the detour with the skip loader as soon as they make the turn, right?"

"You got it."

Minutes seem like hours when you're going into a battle. I don't expect to get another phone call and am surprised when the phone rattles.

"Reardon."

"Mike," Sol says, his voice stressed, "some guy in a red Corvette just roared past me going at least a hundred."

"Don't sweat it. We'll handle it if it becomes a problem. You spin it around and beat a trail."

"Got it. Hate it, but got it."

In minutes my phone vibrates again, and before I can say hello, Dallas yells into it. "The Cad and a van are on the gravel...and some asshole in a Corvette. We couldn't get in his way."

"Get the hell out of Dodge," I yell back, and take up a position awaiting the oncoming vehicles. The guy in the Vette shouldn't be a speeder. He's on his own.

The Caddi's in the lead. I put the first one through the radiator at a hundred fifty yards, then one into the driver's side tire. The big black Cad jerks left, then straightens by the time I bolt the third .308 into the chamber, and that one goes into the passenger side front tire.

By this time it seems they get wise to the fact that someone is firing at them and slide to a stop.

The van has to stop behind them, and I put one into the passenger side front tire but can't see the driver's side as the Cad's in the way, so I flatten the passenger side rear.

By this time the blonde guy, Fitor, the driver of the pickup loaded with explosives that wiped out Pax's place, has made my location and is firing a semi-auto handgun out the passenger side window, reaching across Ahmeti to do so.

I have no problem putting the crosshairs on Fitor, but before I can squeeze one off, a burst sprays the windshield coming from Skip's position. The front of the Cad goes still as Ahmeti must be hiding as low as he can get.

The rear of the van slides open and out pile two guys, one of them runs for the brush at the roadside but the other drops to a knee and begins spraying Skip's side of the hill with an automatic pistol...looks like an Uzi from my distant position.

I swing the .308 crosshairs on him and center punch him. His arms windmill as he rocks back against the van then slumps. The two guys in the front of the van are hunkered down and have the van in reverse, trying to get the hell back the way they came, when the red Corvette, its top down, roars up behind and brakes hard, almost sliding into the rear.

I can see the Vette guy stand up in the front seat to look out over the windshield, I'm sure wondering what the hell the noise is. Then I swear, even from over a hundred yards, I see his eyes widen and he drops down as the driver of the van runs back and tries to catch up with him. I guess the van driver is wanting a ride out of trouble, but the Vette guy is too fast and dirt flies from the rear tires as he spins the wheels, getting the hell out of there. The driver is running after him, waving his arms, but to no avail.

The driver realizes he's not gonna get a ride and runs off the road into the weeds.

I don't recognize him, so I let him go.

The last guy in the van is out of sight, probably retreated to the rear.

Ahmeti, who's promised to whack Pax and me, and whom I'm sure is a man of his word, has climbed behind the wheel of the Cad and is trying to drive forward on two flat tires. Just for the hell of it I put another one into the radiator, then another in the rear passenger side tire. He's making a little headway, none the less, but damn little.

If my count is right we've got a guy in the weeds, another guy still in the back of the van, and Ahmeti behind the wheel of the Cad trying to make a getaway vehicle out of what's now little more than a boulder in the middle of the road. It's moving, but about two miles an hour. The original driver of the Cad, Fitor, is face down in the road, I hope hurting real bad and dying real slow. One of the van guys is running for Needles. One of the van guys is still in the back of the van. One of the van guys is face down in the road thanks to my .308.

So there are only three threats left.

Ahmeti has decided the Cad won't get him out of danger and is climbing out. Unlike his partner, Gashi, this guy has no fat on him. He's at least my height, maybe an inch taller at six-foot-three, and moves gracefully, like he might have been a real athlete in his youth. He feints like he's going to run on up the road, which would put him even closer to us, but then breaks back. Only then do I realize the trunk lid is rising. He's popped the latch from the inside, and he disappears behind the lid at the rear of the car.

Then he comes up with what looks like an AK47...he doesn't get the bolt thrown before I nail him high in the chest the same time I hear a three shot blast from Skip's M4. Ahmeti reels back at least ten feet and bounces off the front of the van and goes to his face in the gravel.

Four down, two to go. I have no interest in blowing the van all to hell as it's full of the dough, presuming that's what's in the suitcases Sol saw them load, but a demonstration might just get the guy out of the weeds and the other one out of the back of the van.

I drop the .308 and unsling my M4, better for close work, and advise Skip I'm moving in. I zig and zag down the hill until I'm only fifty yards from the vehicles and the bush where one guy is hiding, and yell out. "I got no bone to pick with you guys. Only two of you left, one in the brush, one in the back of the van. Throw down your weapons and come on out."

Nothing. Not a peep.

So I yell again. "I have enough Semtex out here to blow you guys back to Laughlin, and will if you don't give it up. Throw your weapons out in the road."

Still no sound. I grab my iPhone and open the app that controls the Parrot mini drone, one of the two I've hidden by the road, and guide it out onto the gravel road. I roll it up to about twenty five feet behind the van and advise Skip. "I'm about to give them a taste of Semtex to see if we can pry some weapons out of them."

"I'm holding my ears," comes back.

I dial in the number of the phone-activated detonator and the explosion almost lifts the back of the van off the road. I wait until their ears might have time to recover, then yell again, "I got more where that came from. Look out the back of the van." I activate the other Parrot drone and roll it out into the road, about fifty feet behind the van and let it set, ominous with the yellow-orange blob of Semtex stuck to the top of its video camera like a cancerous growth. Then I activate the quad copter, and lift it off and maneuver it over the thicket of brush where I know one of them is hiding, and actually spot him via the GoPro and the real time monitor on the iPhone, then I maneuver it behind the van until it's hovering only six feet from the back at window height.

I can hear the van door open, and flare the quad copter away and quickly gain a hundred feet of altitude so the a-hole doesn't shoot my toy down.

But then a heavily accented voice rings out. "I am throwing my weapon out. Do not shoot."

"Out on the road, then you walk at least twenty paces from it and lay down, face down, arms and legs spread."

And he moves out. It's the fat guy who was sleeping when he was supposed to be guarding Skip and Tammy. I'm surprised Skip doesn't blow him away as soon as we see who it is.

Then, foolish as it is, the other guy bursts from the thicket, spraying gunfire my way, and the ground around me is erupting in plumes of sand.

Then he, too, reverses direction, wind-milling his arms, his AK flying away.

Skip runs up beside me. "You're getting slow, old man," he chides.

"I saw him from the quad copter and he was hunkered down in a shallow cut. I didn't think he could move that fast."

"There you go," Skip said with a grin, "Thinking again. I gotta go give that fat fuck a few kicks as pay back."

"You're bleeding, you're hit in the side," I say, noticing the growing bloom of blood on his side, a little surprised as he's wearing his vest.

"It's not my side. He creased me on the inside of my arm."

Then I see, the blood is flowing pretty freely from a deep graze on the inside of his left bicep. "That needs a compress then stitches."

"I'll bind it with something. We gotta roll. But not before I kick the shit out of fat boy. Payback time."

"Good, I'll check the van for the loot, then let's haul ass out of here. We're not so far from the highway that all this gunfire won't be heard."

Skip heads for where the fat man is spread eagle on the gravel and I palm my Glock and open the side slider on the van. As Sol reported, there are some rifle cases, hard-sided and each built for two weapons, and four of those oversized hard suitcases with wheels, the size a lady might take if she were to be traveling for a month. I hoist each of them and figure them for fifty pounds, then pop the latch on one. Nothing but hundreds, and if I'm any judge there's more than two and a half mil in each. Maybe as much as three mil in each. I consolidate half the contents of one suitcase into the other three, then step out of the van to see that Skip is making fat boy remove his pants and shoes.

I speak to him via the radio. "You into fat guys now."

"I'm into making the fat fuck walk on this hot gravel barefoot if he wants to get back to the road."

"Then send him on his way." And he does, the fat man begins a comical hot foot hobble back toward the highway, at least a half mile away.

"Skip, stay with the money. We're leaving the light suitcase, with over a mil, so the cops will think this was something other than a robbery. Hang tight. I'm going after the van. I'll have to reload the Harley so I'll be a while."

I leave the M4 as it'll weigh me down and I have to retrieve the .308, and chug up the hill. I'm back in twenty minutes, driving the van right down the slope doing a little boney-bouncing. Just to add to the collection and as we'll have to get rid of the weapons we've used, we take their AK47s and one nice Heckler Koch and place our M4's in strategic locations. Some CSI guys will have a grand old time trying to figure out which of the weapons shot which bad guy and from where.

And we're off to Quartzsite, with what I hope is at least ten mil in the back of the van, to make this little adventure come to a conclusion.

After I get Skip to someone who'll stitch him up.

179

Target Shy & Sexy

Chapter Twenty-Six

I get the hell out of Dodge and away from the scene of the multi-crimes as quickly as possible, but then stop in Vidal Junction to pull into the truck stop parking lot and dig out my medical kit. I could stitch Skip up myself and have the sutures to do so, but I'm afraid the bullet nicked a vein or artery the way he's bleeding and that's beyond my ken, so I bind the hell out of it, hopefully not cutting off the blood supply. Then I decide I have to take a slight detour through Blythe. To have him patched up properly.

It's almost fifty miles to Blythe, and he's still weeping blood even with the tight bandages by the time we get there and find an emergency room.

And I'm running short of time.

I drop Skip off in front of Palo Verde Hospital, a small facility in the small town of Blythe.

"I'm not waiting—"

"Bullshit," he snaps.

"You're going to have to give them some B.S. regarding how you got that wound. I'd suggest you tell him it was a hunting accident and you were pulling your rifle out of the back seat and it went off. Now get in there and let me get out of here."

"Bullshit, you wait. At least leave me the Harley."

"I can't, Skip. I might need the bike and we don't have time for an interrogation by some hillbilly sheriff. I'll be back."

"Okay, okay, I'll handle this. You be careful."

"10-4," I say and as soon as he steps out of the van, I'm out of there. It's only twenty-five miles, east, to Quartzsite, Arizona, and my hoped-for rendezvous with Edvin Gashi.

A quick check of the time on my iPhone tells me he's due there in an hour to pick up his dough from his ex-partner. And ex is the right word, as he's exited this earth.

I should have a half hour to get set up once I find the airport, and that should be easy in a berg like Quartzsite. Most of the snowbirds who frequent the town in the winter should have flown the coup by now, at least I hope so as the fewer folks who might get caught by a stray bullet, the better.

Using Siri to dial, I get Sol, who answers on the first half of the first ring. "How's it going?" he asks.

"Good, we discouraged a few guys but I may have screwed up by leaving a couple who could make some phone calls and maybe cancel the meeting I have scheduled. Any way you can track phone calls from there."

"I might, given enough time. I'd have to get in the carrier's system and I'd have to know what number I'm looking for."

"No chance. I'll have to wing it. Odds are a call won't go through to an aircraft."

"That depends."

"Yeah, I know, I'm flying blind. Are you back in Laughlin?"

"Not quite."

"Hang there in case I need something. I had to leave Skip in Blythe…he…he hurt himself."

"Bad?"

"No, but it had to be taken care of. Stand by. If you don't hear from me in an hour, call him and tell him you're coming to get him."

"I'll hear from you. Be careful."

"10-4, you stand by."

I stop at the main crossroads in Quartzsite and get directions to the only airport around. Of course as I look around, the whole of my surroundings may be the world's largest airstrip as the desert is flat with some vegetation and only a few ravines. It's a rock collectors heaven, however, but there are a thousand places to land a small STOL, short takeoff and landing, aircraft.

I'm a little surprised to see a fairly short airport with both ends of the strip x'ed out, which means it's not kosher to land there. Like Gashi gives a big rat's ass. There is, however, a wind sock and the wind is pushing it around. It should tell me which way these guys are landing.

There's one small metal building, and one car parked nearby. A web search has said there's no fixed base operator and no radio control. The wind is out of the northwest, so I head for the north end of the strip as they'll land into the wind. The paving is short enough that any plane landing there will have to use up most the strip, and then will have to dodge the potholes. They sure as hell are not flying a Citation into this shithole, more likely a 210 or something even smaller.

Now, if only Gashi is aboard.

I position myself three quarters of the way down the strip, hiding the van in a nearby ravine that only hides about the bottom half, take both the M4 and the .308 and move up near the strip and find a comfortable spot at the base of a thin screw-bean mesquite, and decide that's my makeshift hidey hole. Just in case something happens to me, I haul the suitcases of dough up the ravine a hundred fifty yards until I find a place where the bank is deeply undercut and I can hide the suitcases and jump up and down on the bank and collapse it and hide the goodies. Then I return to my poor excuse for a hidey hole.

And my wait is not long. The aircraft makes a flyby and I recognize it as a Comp Air 7, single engine, but STOL and with a good payload. I know this airplane as a lot of guys who want to land where no one else does, or can, use it. She's turbine powered with over six hundred horses, balloon tired and can get in and out of places few planes can. And she has a big payload of a ton, plenty for three or four guys and twelve mil in hundreds.

I can't tell how many guys are aboard, or if the fat man is among them. I guess the pilot is merely checking the wind direction.

They make a wide sweeping turn, I guess checking the area for vehicles, and I know they can see the van as its white will stand out clearly in the desert.

I have absolutely no interest in killing some poor sap who's been hired to fly these guys, and hope it doesn't come to me having to abort to avoid doing so. He makes a long approach and touches down, and I lay the .308 on the fat tire on my side of the strip. He slows, and slows, until he's only a hundred yards from my position.

Squeezing one off, the .308 bucks in my hands, the tire goes flat, and the plane swerves my way and rolls to a stop. The sun is reflecting off the windscreen so I still can't tell who's on board. I'm going to feel pretty stupid if I've just risked some mining company's plane ground looping and killing everyone on board.

But my doubts are quickly squashed as guys pile out of both sides and the guy coming out the pilot's side is carrying an automatic pistol with a thirty shot clip and as soon as he hits the tarmac is firing. But he doesn't see me and is shooting at what's showing of the van. But I'm not so lucky with the guy who comes out of the passenger side. He lays the barrel of another weapon across the wing strut and dirt kicks up all around my location. I should have had a flash suppressor on the .308 as he made my location. I keep my belly and my face in the dirt until he has to change the clip. Then pop up and, I think, drop him center-punched with a .308. But before I can correct to the other guy, that one's on me and spraying my location. Again, I'm eating dirt.

When he runs his clip out I rise up and to my surprise, the first guy, who must have been wearing a vest, is shouldering an RPG. These guys came ready to play for keeps. I'm six feet from the edge of the ravine, and spring backwards until I fall over the edge and am three feet lower than the surface.

The explosion, at my former location, does not spray me with shrapnel, but does rock my world and my ears are getting nothing but a shrill ringtone. I move twenty feet down the ravine, unsling the Heckler Koch I've taken from the other bad guys, and come up over the edge with a sweep of fire that should get their attention, only to see the guy with the RPG being loaded. We fire at the same time, only this time he's not firing at me and I drop again and turn to see my van go up in a cloud of smoke and fire.

Damn it, my ride, and not only my ride, but my second ride. My Harley Iron is now scrap metal. I wish I had left it for Skip.

Damn, damn, damn if that doesn't piss me off. I switch the clip around and come back up to see both guys outside the aircraft are down. And not moving.

I hope, hope, hope that fat man Gashi is in the back of the aircraft, and move to where I can't be seen by anyone inside and approach from directly in front as the Comp Air 7 is a tail dragger and the long nose hides me.

When I'm close enough, and as no one has appeared, I side step with the Heckler Koch on my shoulder and see no one else in the plane. I move on up and do a quick check to make sure no one is hiding in the rear, and no one is.

Two guys down on the tarmac and that's it. Gashi has sent a trusted aide to pick up his dough.

I wipe down my weapons then put my Glock in the hands of one of the dead guys and my .308 in the other guy's grip, and take their weapons. The long gun is an AK47 and the auto pistol an Uzi. The cops will have a hell of a time figuring out who shot who and why.

Gashi, who wants to kill us, is still out there somewhere.

And if he wanted to kill us before, he must be a madman now that we have his dough. And I'll bet he figures out who picked his pocket.

So, my next job is lined up for me. Find and finish Edvin Gashi, if I have to chase him all the way to Albania. I don't like having to watch my six at all times.

I go back and make sure the dough is well hidden, ditch all my weapons and accouterments including my Kevlar vest, in the desert at the first badger hole a quarter mile from the airport, then start hoofing it out of there in earnest before the badges show up…if anyone even heard the gunfire. I can hear the ammunition going off in the burning van I'm leaving behind, then the crack of my stash of flash and fragmentation grenades. If the cops don't hear that, I'll be very surprised.

I'll have to call it in stolen as soon as I hit Vegas, and, of course, deny knowledge of any of the tricks of my trade that the van contains…damn it.

On my way, I call Sol and ask him to head for the hospital in Blythe, where, with luck I'll find a way to get to before the cops start looking for a perp. It's a two-mile walk to the Grubstake Social Club so I make it at a hustle, and, by the time I arrive a half hour later, have still not heard sirens. There's a service station with a store attached and I stop and buy myself a tee shirt, "Geologists know Schist" which I presume is some kind of mineral. Now I look like a local, or at least a snowbird who comes to hunt rocks. I find the men's room and change, leaving my camo shirt in the trash.

I make the saloon and decide to take the time to clear the gun smoke out of my throat with a Jack Daniels on the rocks, and as luck would have it, there's a freckle faced redhead who looks much better in her tee shirt than I do in mine, not to speak of the skin tight leggings. And she's only two stools from me, so I sidle up.

"How you doing?"

She stares straight ahead. "Great, not that it's any of your business," she says.

"Jesus, girl, what's in your pretty little craw?"

"Men."

"Okay, I'll turn on my feminine side."

That almost gets a smile out of her, and at least she turns to face me.

I give her my most harmless smile, and raise my voice an octave. "And, as one girl to another, I'll buy us a drink."

That earns a smile.

So I charge forward. "Now, girlfriend, tell me about this son of a bitch who did you wrong."

And that gets a laugh, and I'm encouraged as she looks me up and down, as I've already done to her and liked what I saw. "I left the prick in Phoenix."

"Crying his eyes out, suicidal I'm sure."

She laughs again.

"Okay," she says, "I give, you can go back to being what you so obviously are."

"Which is?" A smart guy, like a good trial attorney, never asks a question when he's not sure of the answer, but I like her answer none-the-less.

Her voice gets a little husky. "All man, I'd guess."

"You, girl, are a good guesser. Is there someplace around here I can buy us some supper."

"Can't do it."

"Don't break my heart this early in our budding relationship."

"I'm heading for Blythe and just stopped for a beer. My mom is waiting to console me."

There is a God.

A Look at *Judge, Jury, Desert Fury*, the next book in The Repairman Series

Back in the fray, only this time it's as a private contractor. Mike Reardon and his buddies are hired to free a couple of American's held captive by a Taliban mullah, and, as usual, it's duck, dodge and kick ass when everyone in the country wants a piece of you. Don't miss this high action adventure by renowned author L. J. Martin. No. 6 in The Repairman series, each book stands alone.

Other Fine Action Adventure from L. J. Martin

West of the War

Young Bradon McTavish watches the bluecoats brutally hang his father and destroy everything he's known, and he escapes their wrath into the gunsmoke and blood of war. Captured and paroled, only if he'll head west of the war, he rides the river into the wilds of the new territory of Montana where savages and grizzlies await. He discovers new friends and old enemies...and a woman formerly forbidden to him.

<u>Windfall</u>. From the boardroom to the bedroom, David Drake has fought his way...nearly...to the top. From the jungles of Vietnam, to the vineyards of Napa, to the grit and grime of the California oil fields, he's clawed his way up. The only thing missing is the woman he's loved most of his life. Now, he's going to risk it all to win it all, or end up on the very bottom where he started. This business adventure-thriller will leave you breathless.

<u>Bloodlines</u>. When an ancient document is found deep under the streets of Manhattan, no one can anticipate the wild results. A businessman is forced to search deep into his past and reach back to those who once were wronged, and redeem for them what is

right and just. There's a woman he's yearned for, and must have, but all is against them…and someone want him dead.

The Repairman. No. 1 on Amazon's crime list! Got a problem? Need it fixed? Call Mike Reardon, the repairman, just don't ask him how he'll get it done. Trained as a Recon Marine to search and destroy, he brings those skills to the tough streets of America's cities. If you like your stories spiced with fists, guns, and beautiful women, this is the fast paced novel for you.

The Bakken No. 1 on Amazon's crime list! The stand alone sequel to The Repairman. Mike Reardon gets a call from his old CO in Iraq, who's now a VP at an oil well service company in

North America's hottest boomtown, and dope and prostitution is running wild and costing the company millions, and the cops are overwhelmed. If you have a problem, and want it fixed, call the repairman…just don't ask him what he's gonna do.

G5, Gee Whiz When a fifty million dollar G5 is stolen and flown out of the country, who you gonna call? If you have a problem, and want it fixed, call the repairman…just don't ask him what he's gonna do.

Who's On Top   Mike Reardon thinks his new gig, finding an errant daughter of a NY billionaire will be a laydown...how wrong can one guy be? She's tied up with an eco-terrorist group, who proves to be much more than that. And this time, the group he's up against may be bad guys, or kids with their heart in the right place. Who gets lead and who gets a kick in the backside. And if things go wrong, the whole country may be at risk! Another kick-ass Repairman Mike Reardon thriller from acclaimed author L. J. Martin.

Target Shy & Sexy What's easier for a search and destroy guy than a simple bodyguard gig, particularly when the body being guarded is on of America's premiere country singers and the body is knockdown beautiful...until she's abducted while he's on his way to report for his new assignment. Who'd have guessed that the hunt for his employer would lead him into a nest of hard ass Albanians and he'd find himself between them and some bent nose boys from Vegas! Another in the highly acclaimed The Repairman Series...Mike Reardon is at it again.

<u>Judge, Jury, Desert Fury.</u> Back in the fray, only this time it's as a private contractor. Mike
Reardon and his buddies are hired to free a couple of American's held captive by a Taliban mullah, and, as usual, it's duck, dodge and kick ass when everyone in the country wants a piece of you. Don't miss this high action adventure by renowned author L. J. Martin. No. 6 in The Repairman series, each book stands alone.

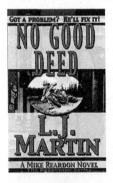

<u>No Good Deed.</u> Going after some ruthless kidnappers, who want NATO,s secrets, is one thing...going into Russia is another altogether. But when one of Reardon's crew is being held, he says to hell with it, no matter if he's risking starting World War 3! Why not add the CIA and the State Department to your list of

enemies when your most important job is staying alive hour by hour, minute by minute.

Overflow. Mike Reardon, the Repairman, hates to mess his own nest—to work anywhere near where he lives. If you can call a mini-storage and a camper living. But when terrorists bomb Vegas, and a casino owner's granddaughter is killed…the money is too good and the prey is among his most hated. Then again nothing is ever quite like it seems. Now all he has to do is stay alive, tough when friends become enemies and enemies far worse, and when you're on top the FBI and LVPD's list.

Quiet Ops. "...knows crime and how to write about it...you won't put this one down." Elmore Leonard
L. J. Martin with America's No. 1 bounty hunter, Bob Burton, brings action-adventure in double doses. From Malibu to West Palm Beach, Brad Benedick hooks 'em up and haul 'em in...in chains.

Crimson Hit. Dev Shannon loves his job, travels, makes good money, meets interesting
people...then hauls them in cuffs and chains to justice. Only this time it's personal.

Bullet Blues. Shannon normally doesn't work in his hometown, but this time it's a friend who's gone missing, and he's got to help...if he can stay alive long enough. Tracking down a stolen yacht, which takes him all the way to Jamaica, he finds himself deep in the dirty underbelly of the drug trade.

The Clint Ryan Series:

El Lazo. John Clinton Ryan, young, fresh to the sea from Mystic, Connecticut, is shipwrecked on the California coast…and blamed for the catastrophe. Hunted by the hide, horn and tallow captains, he escapes into the world of the vaquero, and soon gains the name El Lazo, for his skill with the lasso. A classic western tale of action and adventure, and the start of the John Clinton Ryan, the Clint Ryan series.

Against the 7th Flag. Clint Ryan, now skilled with horse and reata, finds himself caught up in the war of California revolution, Manifest Destiny is on the march, and he's in the middle of the fray, with friends on one side and countrymen on the other…it's fight or be killed, but for whom?

The Devil's Bounty. On a trip to buy horses for his new ranch in the wilds of swampy Central California, Clint finds himself compelled to help a rich Californio don who's beautiful daughter has been kidnapped and hauled to the barracoons of the Barbary Coast. Thrown in among the Chinese tongs, Australian Sidney Ducks, and the dredges of the gold rush failures, he soon finds an ally in a slave, now a newly freedman, and it's gunsmoke and flashing blades to fight his way to free the senorita.

<u>The Benicia Belle</u>. Clint signs on as master-at-arms on a paddle wheeler plying the Sacramento from San Francisco to the gold fields. He's soon blackmailed by the boats owner and drawn to a woman as dangerous and beautiful as the sea he left behind. Framed for a crime he didn't commit, he has only one chance to exact a measure of justice and…revenge.

<u>Shadow of the Grizzly</u>. "Martin has produced a landlocked, Old West version of Peter Benchley's *Jaws*," Publisher's Weekly. When the Stokes brothers, the worst kind of meat hunters, stumble on Clint's horse ranch, they are looking to take what he has. A wounded griz is only trying to stay alive, but he's a horrible danger to man and beast. And it's Clint, and his crew, including a young boy, who face hell together.

11

Condor Canyon. On his way to Los Angeles, a pueblo of only one thousand, Clint is ambushed by a posse after the abductor of a young woman. Soon he finds himself trading his Colt and his skill for the horses he seeks...now if he can only stay alive to claim them.

The Montana Series – The Clan:

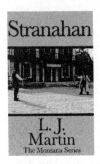

Stranahan. "A good solid fish-slinging gunslinging read," William W. Johnstone. Sam Stranahan's an honest man who finds himself on the wrong side of the law, and the law has their own version of right and wrong. He's on his way to find his brother, and walks into an explosive case of murder. He has to make sure justice is done...with or without the law.

<u>McCreed's Law</u>. Gone…a shipment of gold and a handful of passengers from the Transcontinental Railroad. Found…a man who knows the owlhoots and the Indians who are holding the passengers for ransom. When you want to catch outlaws, hire an outlaw…and get the hell out of the way.

<u>Wolf Mountain</u>. The McQuades are running cattle, while running from the tribes who are fresh from killing Custer, and they know no fear. They have a rare opportunity, to get a herd to Mile's and his troops at the mouth of the Tongue…or to die trying. And a beautiful woman and her father, of questionable background, who wander into camp look like a blessing, but trouble is close on their trail…as if the McQuades don't have trouble enough.

<u>O'Rourke's Revenge</u>. Surviving the notorious Yuma Prison should be enough trouble for any man...but Ryan O'Rourke is not just any man. He wants blood, the blood of those who framed him for a crime he didn't commit. He plans to extract revenge, if it costs him all he has left, which is less than nothing...except his very life.

<u>McKeag's Mountain</u>. Old Bertoldus Prager has long wanted McKeag's Mountain, the Lucky Seven Ranch his father had built, and seven hired guns tried to take it the hard way, leaving Dan McKeag for dead...but he's a McKeag, and clings to life. They should have made sure...for now it will cost them all, or he'll die trying, and Prager's in his sights as well.

The Nemesis Series:

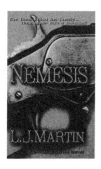

Nemesis. The fools killed his family...then made him a lawman! There are times when it pays not to be known, for if they had, they'd have killed him on the spot. He hadn't seen his sister since before the war, and never met her husband and two young daughters...but when he heard they'd been murdered, it was time to come down out of the high country and scatter the country with blood and guts.

Mr. Pettigrew. Beau Boone, starving, half a left leg, at the end of his rope, falls off the train in the hell-on-wheels town of Nemesis. But Mr. Pettigrew intervenes. Beau owes him, but does he owe him his very life? Can a one-legged man sit shotgun in one of the toughest saloons on the Transcontinental. He can, if he doesn't have anything to lose.

The Ned Cody Series:

Buckshot.   Young Ned Cody takes the job as City Marshal…after all, he's from a long line of lawmen. But they didn't face a corrupt sheriff and his half-dozen hard deputies, a half-Mexican half-Indian killer, and a town who thinks he could never do the job.

Mojave Showdown. Ned Cody goes far out of his jurisdiction when one of his deputies is hauled into the hell's fire of the Mojave Desert by a tattooed Indian who could track a deer fly and live on his leavings. He's the toughest of the tough, and the

Mojave has produced the worst. It's ride into the jaws of hell, and don't worry about coming back.

About the Author

L. J. Martin is the author of over 30 book-length works from such major NY publishers as Bantam, Avon, and Pinnacle. His works of fiction include westerns, thrillers, mysteries, and historicals. His non-fiction includes a book on killing cancer (he's a two-time cancer survivor), a cookbook, a how-to book on writing, a book of cartoons, and a political thesis. Many of his recent titles have been best sellers on the Number 1 bookseller in the world, Amazon. His avocations include photography (with over 100 videos on Youtube—see ljmartinwolfpack), cooking (see wolfpackranch.com), travel, gardening, shooting, fishing and hunting. L. J. lives in Montana with his wife, Kat, a NYT bestselling, internationally published author of over 55 historical and romantic suspense novels.

Made in the USA
Coppell, TX
01 September 2020

35085874R00125